Monsieur

An Anthology of Novellas-in-Flash

Edited by
Gaynor Jones

Copyright © 2022 The authors and Retreat West Books
Print Edition

First published by Retreat West Books in 2022

Apart from use permitted by UK copyright law, this publication may only be reproduced, stored, or transmitted, in any for, or by any means, with prior permission by email of the publishers; or in the case of reprographic production in accordance with the terms of license issued by the Copyright Licensing Agency.

ISBN eBook: 978-1-9196087-6-1
ISBN print: 978-1-9196087-7-8

Retreat West Books
retreatwest.co.uk/books

Contents

***Monsieur* by David Rhymes**	1
A Libertine	3
Original Sin	5
We Kiss for the First Time	7
Had I Been Born a Man	9
Plant Lore	11
Fieldwork	13
Blood in the Mountains	15
The Monks of Chartreuse	17
Paris	19
Buffon's Proposal	21
Preparation	23
Departure and After	25
Madeira	28
Matters of Privilege	31
The Naturalists	33
Vivès Again	35
Crossing the Line	38
Turk's Man	40
Life Below Decks	43
Tahiti	45
Vahine	47
Tattoo	49
Unmasked	51
Mauritius, one year later	52

***Ceiling* by Hannah Sutherland**	55
Limitless	57
Limited	59
Wall	60
Air	63
House	65
Blind	67
Roots	68
Missing	70
Unspoken rules	71
Awake	74
Daisy Chains	77
Home	79
Slipping Through Her Fingers	81
Happy	83
Tattie Sheds	85
Heirloom	87
Outside But In	88
Heavy	90
Different	91
Lost at Sea	93
Oh Da Oh Da Oh Da	94
Goodbye	96
Normal	97
Entwined	98
Ceiling	100
***The Girl Who Survived* by Dawn Siofra North**	103
Part One	105
Casting Off	107
Seeking	108

Tower	110
The Promise	111
Threshold	114
Thin Air	115
Sparkling	117
Ten Tall Tales That Gabriel Has Told Me	118
Journal of Incalculable Loss, Author Unknown	120
One life in a list	122
Exchange	125
Small Hope	128
Part Two	129
Spellbroken	131
Crush	133
Hush	136
Inheritance	139
Homecoming	142
Beyond	144
Surrender	147
Part Three	149
Creation	151
Volunteers Needed: Must be willing to tend pain	154
Temporary Safety	157
The Crossing	159
The Authors	163

Monsieur

David Rhymes

A Libertine

I TELL MONSIEUR that if I were a man, I'd be a libertine, immune to the chains of propriety – like old Voltaire, with whom he stayed, a full year in Geneva, surviving on a diet of spartan roots and brandy, talking rights and privileges, debating the true age of the earth. I'd be the type who'd think herself immune to censure, a little like you, I say, inspecting with the aid of an enlarging glass the pink tips of his nipples six times life.

'You're quite the rascal, Jeanne,' he says, inviting me to straddle him and bounce about in his lap, grasping tight the pink whorls of his ears, a little clumsily it's true, for we've been drinking absinthe and my head is fuzzy, my fingers sticky with the juice of oysters', slapdash in the sluice of love.

We are together in the hothouse, naked as the day: Madame is somewhere in the house, her heavy belly fat as the full moon, with little Archambeau about to slip between her legs into this wretched and uneven earth. But still, we toast her absence, our good fortune, quite as carelessly as sunbeams fête the air, engaging in depravity, and caring not one jot, because one must – in this unequal world – be free.

Original Sin

WE MET FOR the first time at the rear gate of his house in Chalaronne. Monsieur took hold of my hand and he led me gently through the green parterre towards the hothouse, saying he would need more wheatgrass, valerian, and eyebright.

'Have you brought yarrow, and fresh bay leaf? Oh – and I will need a little feverfew.'

I took each seed wrap from my basket, laid them on the sorting counter ready for the corresponding phial or jar. This was the business I was born to, raised to know which herbs were valued, where they grew, their properties and use. The price at which they should purvey.

'Have you brought any sachets of Swiss tea?'

'Of course.' This rich concoction, distilled from twenty herbs, was known to mitigate most toothaches, lumbagos, and gout. A *mélange* valued all about the country, not only by Monsieur.

'Your mother's recipe, I think, Jeanne?'

'Yes, sir, it is.'

'And you, my dear – why come alone? Does your

mother not walk out with you now?'

'She's attending to the apothecaries, sir.'

'Ah! So, you have permission to be here alone? Does she not think you might come to harm, a girl so inexperienced, unchaperoned?'

'No, sir, she asked me to come here.'

'She warned you to take care I expect?'

'Yes, sir.' Although the truth was that my mother said this man was ripe fruit primed to fall. It was her wish that I might seek a route out of the drudgery of our shared life, and she had sent me there on purpose, like a baited hook.

'Perhaps,' she said, 'Since he, the naturalist at Chalaronne, is rich as Croesus and a fool for flesh, a libertine to boot, you'll have your chance. So go to him alone. And make yourself...*agreeable.*'

She pinned and tucked my Sunday gown, connived to make remarkable my hips, my bust. 'If you work properly,' she said, fresh hairpins fixed betwixt her teeth, 'he lifts you out of drudgery. You lose something, it's true, but also you will gain a life.' Braiding my hair, scenting my throat with lavender, she said. 'Now go. You know your purpose, girl.'

Like saffron traded for a guinea, I complied.

We Kiss for the First Time

CONVEYED BY MONSIEUR'S touch on my elbow into his private quarters, there to sit, I crouched demurely on a stool, unsure how I might force this vital change upon the world my mother had in mind. I was a ship suspended in a windless sea – lacking a means of propulsion, without experience of any kind.

'Do you drink wine?'

'Yes, sir.'

'Do you like oysters raw? Have you tried those?'

'No, sir.'

'Then we shall have a dozen on the half shell here. Come. Sit beside me on this green divan. Watch how I do it, Jeanne, with one clean fluid sucking motion, thus, clearing the conch without interference, either from tooth or jaw.'

I copied him, a little disgusted it is true, yet complicit in the act.

'Now – let's look through my herbals; you can remind me of some common names and meanings.'

So then, of course, we did just this. And Nature soon

came swiftly to my aid. With my young figure pressing close to his, Monsieur's arm crept around my waist. His fingertips strayed to my thigh. Observing that I didn't flinch or press his hand away, he plucked the wine glass from my hand, laid it away, then slid onto his knees, grasping my hands and sighing, 'Oh, Jeanne!'

And plunging forward, pressed his lips to mine.

Seized by a wherewithal I had not previously suspected was mine, I stood up smartly, stepped out of my skirts and sank my innocence astride the rising point of exclamation in his lap.

Had I Been Born a Man

'HAD I BEEN born a man,' I told Monsieur, when we were lounging in those first louche days of lust, 'I'd not stay put, but stride abroad, go hotfoot over rocks, root out new seeds, rip up new herbs. Set fire to these ridiculous girl's skirts. Don good men's breeches, sturdy boots, a cap. I'd go outside all day and scramble on my knees through the tall grass. I'd hound the lizards from their hides.'

'You should love your life,' Monsieur replied. 'One's sex, as Rousseau says, is not transferable.'

'And yet my life chafes like the bone stays in my gown. My feet ache in my pinch-toe boots. I rage against constraint. I do not fit my life.'

'Ach, Jeanne – why don't we find some better boots and a spare cap and walk about the country, master-and-footman-so-to-speak? We could go foraging together, *in cognito* – you could look at life from the man's side? Would you like that? Would that be nice?'

Of course, I didn't hesitate; I donned a suit of clothes pulled from a footman's trunk and tracked through

Monsieur's garden to the woods. I with shoulders raised, my cap pulled low, he out front and striding *nonchalantly,* two steps forward, pinking the ground with his cane.

In the silent forest, thrilled at the success of this new ruse, we set about the work of observation, collecting, cataloguing nature, lovers become brothers, become equals in the world.

Plant Lore

MONSIEUR SHOWED GREAT interest in the things my mother taught me as a girl. The common names and uses for each plant – each *specimen* to use his word – which we together found. I taught him modes of preservation, mixing, blending; application, mostly medicinal; but also, things of mystery, observing how such things I shared with him beyond the scope of science or religion delighted him, roused eagerness to lick the graphite point and press me to repeat the details so he was able to record them in his notes.

How bracken seed can make a witch invisible.

Why ferns are called the Devil's brush and hang in kitchens to deflect lightning.

How, it is said, you may tie a dog to a mandrake root and place his dinner at a distance, so when he tugs, the shriek will save the man, and slay the dog, but leave the root intact.

I told him yew roots in a graveyard grow up through dead men's eyes, preventing them from spying on the world.

How the elder tree contains the smell of death.

How you must never burn the hawthorn on your hearth, for the Devil will sneak down your chimney and jump into your mouth.

We dug out roots, tubers, rusts and smuts and mildews, Monsieur glazed with astonished eyes at my efficiency – proclaiming he had found in me not only a brother gardener, but a person who could help him in the compilation of an Herbal which, he assured me with much sincerity and faith, would set a new high-water mark within his field.

Fieldwork

IT WAS NOT long after this day that Madame Commerson, his wife, began her confinement. The child was born sickly; the mother seemed likely to die. Monsieur lay weeping in our bed, cradled in my arms, distraught. Although his wife had been a widow well past thirty when he married her for money; and though she held for him but little interest personally; the child was innocent, and so, for a short time, his conscience pricked.

And yet, instead of pining at her bedside, or caring for Archambeau, he plunged his energy more deeply into work. He came to me while I was in the hothouse workshop drying herbs. 'We're leaving Jeanne. You'll need your fieldwork gear.'

'We're going where?'

'To the mountains, Jeanne. To the Alps.'

Conveyed there in a coach and four we soon arrived.

The high peaks formed a long, serrated edge; we trekked on foot together uphill from the road, came inching forward on the ridge. I carried on my shoulders as his servant a broad yoke, a broad wingspan of phials and jars, of curing boxes, cages, traps – the rock hammer, the steel point brush. Silk folds of pins and twine. Stumbling like a mule, back bent, I followed him, my master, uphill to the monastery at old Chartreuse. I walked in his crisp shadow edged to hyperclear in that thin air, that breathless altitude.

The bluff was sheer, pocked with small clumps of alpine plants, bright button flowers. We picked them, pressed them, stored them, fingers trembling, delving into icy clefts of rock.

Why do I long, I asked myself, bent with my burdens while he sprang ahead of me, light on his feet, *to trail behind this man, doing his bidding, silent and obedient, for love?*

Blood in the Mountains

IN THE SNOW and flint of the high Alps, we drove into a blizzard wind. The windows of the coach froze shut, glazed like sugar work, to which my fingertips stayed glued. We got down to pick simples, felt the green stems brittle as we folded them in keeping papers, dabbing at them gently as they thawed.

Near Croissy, Monsieur leapt down alone and strayed into a thicket, tracing bird tracks through the snow.

I stayed behind with the postilion, wrapped in seal furs, watching the ice-melt from the branches, droplets falling muffled into snow, pining for the heat of a good fire.

There came a shout, a snarl, echoing barks, the mad kerfuffle of a dog, a wolf, and a black shadow crossed under the trees, a blur in the half dark, pursued, then felled. Alarmed, the postilion vaulted from his seat, bellowing as he sped into the trees, beating his arms against his side, swinging the lantern violently about his head. For an instant I saw the eyes of a wolf light up in the beam. A silhouetted shape. But then this fearful creature shook into life, bounded away in darkness and was gone.

Fearing the worst, I leapt down from the coach and ran to meet the postilion's gradually advancing form, his panting scarves of breath as he was dragging back my lover's form along the ground.

'Philibert!' I screamed. 'Philibert!'

My lover's body lay against the runner boards. His leg was gashed, had left a smear of red along the snowy ground. I knelt before him, hurrying to bind his wound with strips torn from my underskirts. His head fell forward on his chest, the lips drained blue. I thrust a stick into a tourniquet of cloth to stem the flow of blood.

'Jean-Pierre,' I called to the postilion, he still battling for breath after the burden of his master's weight. 'I'll need you to help me here to lift Monsieur into the coach. Can you do that? Jean-Pierre, I can't do this alone.'

The Monks of Chartreuse

THE MONKS OF La Chartreuse were goodly men whose vows forbade all contact with the female sex. But Monsieur's leg was suppurating, souring in the bindings placed about the wound.

My fear was hydrophobia, for I had seen this condition and knew its signs: the rambling speech, the fearfulness on seeing water. Monsieur's lips were dry, and he was devilish hot, but he refused to drink.

I knew that time was short, that we must act with speed, that I must change again into my fieldwork gear, and gain admittance to that place. I rallied the postilion, bade him to drive the horses hard, despite the snow rails churning the deep snow, the whole coach sliding too – so soon we came outside the walls.

We hammered at the great oak door, and I, commandeering my version of a man's hoarse tone, yelled for the brothers to fetch out a bier and convey my lover's injured body through to the infirmary.

Amazingly, I passed beneath their gaze. My hair bound tight and tucked under a cap, a loose brown cape tossed over my back, in boots purloined out of Monsieur's valise, I was a man. The brothers took me in without demur.

Soon my master's wound was clean, and he was sleeping, so I slipped away from his bedside and hid inside a dark confession box, shivering under the chapel's stone-cold dome, and stripped again and bound my breasts in linen strips. I bound my breasts so tightly I could hardly fill my lungs, but this no mind, for with my chest pressed flat, my chin made sooty with a lick of dust, I felt more confident – I strode out in plain sight.

I passed.

Paris

UPON RECOVERY, ALBEIT Monsieur still a little lame, we left Chartreuse and drove to that great city, Paris. He had received fresh news by messenger from Montsec; a rolled-up letter of appointment to M. Buffon that he clutched in his fist, used as a wand for pointing out the sights. We rode in past the light-glazed grimace that is Notre Dame, crossed silver bridges, over a river rippling with playful light, past the pigeon-speckled roofs and domes, the white sky closing as we wound into the knotted streets. I eked the windows down to either side and filled the coach with the bright sounds and smells of that great city; the bakeries and fruit stalls, the hammerers and sawyers, scented sawdust in the alleys, the dizzy reek of Charpentier perfumer's shop, the dead rag smell of dead men's clothes, the hawkers supplying the living quarters.

We pulled up at a tall dark building, fronted with a balcony of wrought black iron, silent but for doors thrust open on the higher floors, the sound of a small orchestra, of weeping, woe-struck violins.

'This is Buffon's,' Monsieur informed me, gimping

from the footplate to the ground. 'Come, dear, don't be shy. Walk half a pace behind me, please. Speak only if you're spoken to. Don't let yourself be drawn. But really, you look perfect. Very boy-like. Quite the ruse.'

'But Philibert, they'll smoke me at first sight.'

'Not so, my Jeanne. Take this (his case.) Stay two steps back. Behave as a servant and no one here will pay you the slightest heed.'

Yet I was hesitant, I must confess. I had an actor's fear of stepping out on stage. I hadn't been in public as a man since we had sought the monks' relief, their sewing skills, their broth. Inside that silent, hallowed place – where people seldom looked up from their prayers – I'd passed. But would not Paris prove a harder audience to please?

Such were my fears as we rode in, but they were groundless, so it proved, for Paris is a lively, carefree place.

As soon as Monsieur was installed, I went down to the stable yard to see to the horses, and jockey with the stable lads, and cut a dash with snuff. I said, 'Hey, hie you there, Jean-Michel, this bay mare needs re-shoeing, please get to it, all four feet.' And, since my suit was dark, my hair waxed neat, my breasts bound flat under the strips about my torso – I grew confident again. I passed.

Later, glimpsing my reflection in the mirrored hall, I saw looking back at me an elegant young valet, a fart-catcher pressed into service for his man – and felt invincible.

Buffon's Proposal

YES TRULY, ANY fear I might have had was utterly unfounded it would prove. Monsieur Buffon was small and grey, his eyes so clouded up with cataracts that he saw nothing much beyond the point of his own nose. His mind was tangled up in dust; indeed, I do not think he was aware of me at all.

His house was a *menagerie* – a brace of badgers lounged before the fire, six hedgehogs slept in kitchen pots, a dozen wolf cubs chased two dozen chickens round the yard. Jocko, a Capuchin monkey, captured on the Cape, leapt loose about the house.

M. Buffon and Monsieur walked the lanes of the Jardin du Roi, took coffee in the Rue des Boulangers. They dined together at the fashionable Procope; wheresoever they went, so went I, portering Monsieur's cane, his cloak, his overshoes.

'There is a voyage,' Buffon growled, poking in the hemlock beds for snails, digging with the steel point of his cane. 'A Navy captain, Louis Antoine Bougainville, who plans to undertake a voyage to Peru. He'll sail to the

South Seas. If I were younger, I might go.'

'The mission requires a man of our calling?' Monsieur said. 'Or so I am given to understand?'

'Quite so, quite so.'

'And the mission has plentiful finance?'

'I believe they have so, yes. Since Bougainville is rich.'

'Why, then of course I shall apply.'

AND LATER, IN the seclusion of Monsieur's apartments, he expounded this wonderful idea – 'Think of it, Jeanne. We shall be cabinmates. You shall heave my pieces, for, of course, you must do that. To do otherwise would draw to us much unwelcome attention. But then we won't need to separate. Your knowledge will aid me in the field. Your fieldwork skill, familiarity with my methods, my aims. Because you are, of course, quite indispensable to me, you must accompany me. What do you say? Live out your dream, my love.'

'What of your wife?'

'I'll write to her. Tell her it's a matter of professional urgency.'

'We'll be together for how long?'

Monsieur pondered. 'I don't know, but yes, I think one year or two. One there, one back.'

I lay beside him with my heart under the bindings, utterly suffused with love.

Preparation

'BEFORE WE SAIL,' Monsieur told me, 'You'll need to get the measure of a gun. Let me show you the essentials –

'Treasure your weapon. Keep her backside clean. Prefer a military long gun, the Brown Bess, or the Charleville. One that can be readied with a pre-packed powder charge. Study the flintlock to reduce delay between sighting and firing. Practise diligently and soon you'll shoot as quick and straight as any man. This is a true survival art.'

I practiced with a fowling piece – a plain stock single barrel rifle – and felled countless rows of plates and pots.

Those busy nights before we sailed, I ran new lingo through my head. I had to keep my muzzle down. Hang fire. Never go into a field full-cocked. Full cock only once the game has flushed. Always shoot over a partner's head. Know your preferred mix of powder, shot and wadding for the lock. Prefabricate a standard charge in twists of black.

I wandered with Monsieur around the Quarter, purchasing for me a stout two-breasted seaman's jacket, a blue waistcoat with silver buttons, pin-stripe navy breeches, spatterdashes, socks.

We toyed with the notion of a tricorn hat. An article with silver piping round the brim. At last, I settled for a valet's cap. And then, a small concession to vanity, his, not mine – a mesh game bag to sling onto my gun-belt alongside my powder horn.

Departure and After

THE TWO EXPEDITION vessels, *L'Etoile et La Boudeuse,* stood moored at La Rochelle, lit in the falling dark by lanterns fore and aft. *L'Etoile* the leading barque stood further out, *La Boudeuse,* her secondary store ship nearer in. We were to travel on the former, so we took the pilot boat across the wash into the open ocean, the gathering night fog. I heaved my guts in the cross wind, unaccustomed to the ocean's madcap pitch and roll. I would, at that moment, have tossed my cap and shaken loose my hair, revealed myself to be a girl – although I doubt by that late stage this would have made a jot of difference to them, the rowers, much less made them turn for shore. We were irrevocably launched; I could do nothing more but retch.

Albeit soon we came into the calmer waters of our ship's landward side, were swallowed like a bug in *L'Etoile's* dark wooden aura. Her timbers black with tar, her seams caulked full of dead men's rags. I mean to say she stank. Her ropes and rigging were all tar-black too. We scaled in single file the accommodation ladder,

Monsieur with his face as white as mine, drained by the trek across the wash. He went straight below to wash while I attended to the boarding of our equipage.

I shaped my voice to a coarse husk, barked orders to the stevedores. 'Proceed with care! This pallet must remain intact. Those jars of glass and this carboy of spirits must not be smashed.' I did my manly best (that complex notion, *manly* best…!) to fit in with my fellow heavers at the capstan, shouting filthy banter, snorting loudly as a boar.

The crew of the Etoile, the salts, were mainly drawn from lowly stock. Filthy fellows urged by poverty to seek a living on the sea. Amid their number figured a panoply of sea-bound trades – caulkers, carpenters, rope-makers, sailmakers, blacksmiths, cooks. All received me kindly as their fellow man, not questioning my right or status as one more among their number. Monsieur came back on deck and saw me working, then signalled from the Quarterdeck for me to go with him below.

He had secured the captain's cabin for our use, he informed me as we went below, so I, his personal servant, would stand in the shadow of this gift. So I should stow my luggage, in a boxlike anteroom to his own private quarters, under a bunk, that would be mine.

'This is your station, Jeanne,' he said. 'Provisionally at least. But we will lay together in the captain's bed, and you'll have the use of his private commode, avoiding the need to traipse out to the heads.'

'The heads?'

'Are where the seamen go to do their necessaries, Jeanne – there's a species of rudimentary plank that overhangs the bow.'

'But Philibert, what are you telling me? This whole charade is madness.'

Monsieur was smiling, morbidly amused.

Madeira

A FELLOW PASSENGER, the Comte de Nassau-Guillen, latched onto us from the first day. He was a popinjay in search of adventure, and his sweet soul pranced around us gaily like a butterfly in silks and stays.

The King's Astronomer, M. Veron, another supernumerary, who paid for his own passage, and who remained awake each night to take his readings from the stars, was kind to us also. He was a courteous man, most intelligent and kind.

The last of our deck party was to be the ship's Surgeon, Marc-Francois Vivès. A native of Grenoble, Vivès showed himself to be immediately jealous of Monsieur's exalted status. Vivès harboured dreams of running his own country doctor's practice, and he spoke of how his *lowly* status as a ship's sawbones was only temporary, that he was with us in that role so he might save enough to put down an amount as principal upon a future living. How he had not been born with privilege like some men, but in more humble circumstance, yet had, thorough personal sacrifice and industry, climbed out of the sump without any of the advantages of fortune got by birth.

Monsieur seemed, naturally, to embody the privileges Vivès most despised. I – in my role as Monsieur's valet – represented yet more evidence of softness and corruption.

So his rat's eyes fixed on us both from that first day.

AFTER THREE WEEKS of steady sailing, driven by a good south-westerly, we watered at Madeira. The Governor received our party in a wig and pink frockcoat, pink breeches, and silk mules. A monocle was screwed into his eye. He sat in the fort at Funchiale, gazing with a downturned mouth out of a window at our two ships anchored in the bay.

The gentlemen took chairs. His Excellency clicked his fingers and a boy, not more than fifteen years of age, stepped forward with a dome-shaped object over which was draped a cloth.

His Excellency clapped.

The boy withdrew the cloth. Inside the cage a green parakeet began to shriek: *É um prazer, é um plazer.*

The boy silenced the bird with a sharp shout. He spoke to us in perfect French, 'It's our pleasure to welcome you in the name of the King of Portugal to this dominion of the Portuguese crown.' The boy bowed deeply, somewhat comically. 'But His Excellency wishes to enquire about the nature of your business in Madeira.

Are you spies?'

'My learned friends are men of science…' the captain began.

A short dry laugh – the Governor glared in turn at each of us through the round monocle as if aware of our reality for the first time.

'É uma menina, e uma menina!' the parakeet shrieked. *It's a girl! It's a girl!*

With my head bowed I stepped into Monsieur's shadow; I did not look up from the ground again until we reunited with our ship.

Matters of Privilege

VIVÈS DESIRED TO know why he, Monsieur, permitted me, his servant, to remain below while others (such as he) must spend the best part of their day on deck, enduring the hardships of the sun?

Monsieur adlibbed a tale; he claimed my skin, being sensitive to light, would blister on exposure to light rays.

'A most unfortunate state for a fieldworker, sir.'

'Yes, quite so. And a serious setback to my plans.'

'He has been ill?'

'Not seriously, but I wish to reserve his energies, hoping he might prove useful to me later, in the greater ordeal of the tropics. There I will oblige him to wear a visor, or some equivalent protection.'

'I see.' But this yarn had piqued Vivès' pride. 'Why, if this is a matter of health, have you not had him sent to me? Perhaps I could seek an effective remedy?'

Monsieur looked squarely at the man. 'Do you not think, Surgeon Vivès, as a trained physician and apothecary myself, as well as this man's master, that I have not thought about this matter carefully and taken all the necessary steps?'

'Well, yes, I…'

MONSIEUR ASSURED LATER me as we lay abed, how Vivès voiced a most abject apology, then asked, 'Could you not bind his face in calicoes?'

'In calicoes!' he laughed. 'The fool!'

'I don't like it, Philibert. He's smoked us out. I can feel him staring all the time. He knows. I'm certain of it, yes – the way he watches me, those rat's eyes staring at my back.'

'Hush, Jeanne, the man's an imbecile. A manageable fool. He wouldn't dare to force the subject with me now. You leave his pettiness to me. I'll keep you safe, my love, I swear.'

I lay then in my lover's arms, feeling the slow rock of the vessel as we surged towards the tropics, drifting slowly into sleep, with no choice but to trust in fortune's star.

The Naturalists

SOON OUR LITTLE party, *L'Etoile et la Boudeuse,* began tracking south from Rio to the line, the most of us surviving on a paltry and unappetising diet of hard tack and salt beef. The lack of greens had set our teeth loose in our mouths.

By this time, six months out, Monsieur and I were less inclined to seek the solace of each other's arms but lay apart in our shared cabin after dark and rarely thought of love. In fact, we scarcely spoke at all, except over quotidian matters of collecting interest. I pined not for my master's touch, but for fresh fruit. A plate of greens, a cucumber.

A glass of spring water to slake my thirst.

Monsieur was well – despite having grown thin – his leg wound troubled him at times, but he was vigorous, at peace with nature and the world. His presence at the captain's table kept him hearty; what little he could steal for me kept me half so.

Our days went by in harmony, engaged in catching, classifying, master and his faithful servant, only that.

We cast the net and drew in each day's catch, diversity surprising and delighting both. I made notes in a calfskin slip-book, wrote paragraphs of shorthand, described the sea conditions and the hour – a process clarified by many months of disciplined routine.

First the genus, then the class, brief colour notes to help the painters if the specimens were prone to bleach. A wad of kelp we hooked over the side, containing six species of formerly unknown crustacean. Barnacles we chipped from the hull using a blade. A floating Man of War we landed, subdued with a billhook. In this last case, when its full length was drawn out of the sea, all twenty feet of rainbow tentacle, one of its tendrils stung my hand. This left me with a scarlet brand that I wear to this day. A memory of who I was, who I became. We had this creature killed and placed in spirits for its better preservation.

Vivès Again

THE WAKE WAS where there was most life, where most life congregated, drawn by the shadows at the great ship's tail. I leant over the rail watching the dragnets ride, breathing in fresh ozone, feeling weak it's true, but accustomed to the routine of sailing, albeit with one eye trained on Vivès, always there behind me back, watching my every step, eyes tracking my every move.

'Why do you not go forward to the seats of relief, boy?' he asked, standing by me at the rail, smoking idly, overseeing my labours.

'We have a water closet in our cabin,' I said, stepping forward to assist Monsieur, who held out a large fish, dripping, by the gills.

'Jean uses that.' Monsieur turned thence to me, 'Can you gut this?'

I took up the paring knife, sliced down the belly, spilling a hail of blood and innards on the greasy timbers of the quarterdeck.

'You're most fortunate,' Vivès said. 'And you, sir, most generous with respect to your subordinate's needs.

Allowing him to share your pot.'

The hateful curl of his rat's lip, his rodent's cunning plainly sketched.

Monsieur ignored him, went on with his work.

'For the wind that blows under the seats of ease is sufficient to skin your arse.'

'Vivès, can you not find some species of work?' Monsieur asked. 'Can you not see we're busy? Your talk is a distraction, sir.'

'I was speaking to the captain at breakfast,' Vivès continued. 'Sometime soon we'll cross the line. The Equator. The men of the French Navy will expect to perform a ceremony, sir, a dipping thing.'

I kept my head bowed at my work.

'No one's exempt – at least not without the payment of a heavy fine. I've a crate of brandy that I've been saving for the purpose, sir. I shall exempt myself with that – and you, M. Commerson – what excuse will you make?'

Monsieur said he would pay the necessary tax in French doubloons. He asked Vivès once more if he had got no work. 'Perhaps you might be needed in the sickbay?'

'Ah, we gentlemen, shall certainly be safe,' Vivès retorted, his rat's eyes glimmering with spite. 'Though Jean here won't escape the ruse. He'll be stripped down and dragged at speed through the salt drink on the bareback. It's custom, you know, boy. Beyond the Captain's say so, there are no exceptions granted. There'd be suspicion, see.'

I glared at him with my hands clenched, my fingers splashed with fish's blood. The knife hung cold inside my hand. I might have slit his throat if he had spoken one more word. But I stayed mute; I feared to speak at all would only goad him more.

Crossing the Line

WHEN THE DAY of the ceremony arrived, Monsieur feigned illness. I stayed in the cabin, tending to his fever. We heard the tramp of seamen loose about the decks, and then a sharp knock at the door, voices calling too. This passed. I lay trembling in his arms. Again, the footsteps came, then knocks, demands made in coarse French that we come out and show ourselves.

Monsieur lay a finger to his lips. There was more knocking and the tramp of feet receding. We lay in silence through the close heat of day, listening to the racket of the drunk crew's antics overhead, the scrape of a seaman's fiddle, the cries of merrymaking, stamping feet, the crashing sounds of fighting. Finally, the Boatswain's whistle and in sudden silence, cannon fire – three guns.

'It's over,' Monsieur said. 'We're safe.'

'Oh, Philibert, I can't continue thus.' My throat was parched, my bound chest heaving in constriction, struggling to breathe in that coffin of wooden space. 'I was a fool to think I could. We're both fools.'

'Hush, Jeanne, they have forgotten you.'

'Vivès has guessed, I'm sure of it. He knows.'

'But he will never say. He would not dare. The man's a f –'

Then we were frozen by a knock, a voice we recognised.

Turk's Man

CAPTAIN BOUGAINVILLE STOOD wearily outside the door.

'There's a matter, trivial in the extreme, with which to importune you, sir. Surgeon Vivès is insisting that I speak to you on a matter of propriety, regarding the matter of your servant.'

I busied myself folding linen, arranging things around my master's bed.

'It seems,' the captain said, 'that Vivès has taken umbrage with your man's…your servant's…' The captain coughed lightly behind a raised hand. 'Arrangements here, or better said, arrangements you have made for him.'

'If you're speaking of Neptune's tax, Captain Bougainville, of course I have already paid M. Baret's fine in addition to my own. I have been bilious all day, I'm afraid, and he's been rather too busy to take part, attending to me here.'

'Yes, quite. I understand. Though it's not entirely that. Rather, the matter of his status here, specifically, the conditions of his berth.'

I kept on folding linen, afraid to look up.

'I shall be frank with you, sir. M. Vivès considers it improper for your servant to sleep in your cabin. As he quite rightly says, all of the other servants sleep in hammocks on the lower decks. I've considered his opinion and, since I cannot see a reason to discriminate, I feel it necessary to request that you adhere to precedent.'

'But, Captain Bougainville, sir,' Monsieur began. 'What of the matter of my health?'

'This is a matter for Surgeon Vivès, surely?'

'Sir, I –'

The captain looked over Monsieur's shoulder then and addressed me directly. 'You, sir. M. Baret. Are you heeding our conversation? Please make haste young man and gather up your things. You'll accompany the Purser below. He'll show you to your berth.'

'Wait,' Monsieur stepped forward, pulling the captain into the cabin, guiding his elbow, closing the door at his back.

'What is this –?'

'It's time,' Monsieur said then, 'for us to speak in confidence. Jean – M. Baret – please step forward, boy.'

I left my folding, came to stand at Monsieur's side.

'His story is a sorry thing the boy is loath to share, whose confidence I keep, since I am at least partly responsible, since he was in my service at the time, but M. Baret has suffered a great hardship. He was taken captive in my service, sir, by the Turks while we were foraging, on an expedition to the Sea of Marmara. There is no delicate way around this, sir, but whilst in servitude to me, they capped him, sir – they took his baubles, sir, cut them clean away.'

'My God – I'm sorry, sir!'

'This can explain his beardless face, his piping tones, and something of his reluctance to mix too closely with the roughest types.'

'Yes, yes, of course.'

'Jean is a eunuch, sir. He's a Turk's man.'

Life Below Decks

ONCE THE CAPTAIN left us, I lay in my cot and wept. I couldn't see how we could keep our intrigue safe. We would soon pass into the straits of Magellan and into the Pacific, on the far side of the World. This was a full year's sailing from my home – and now, despite the captain's sympathy, he'd left us with renewed insistence that I take up a servant's berth below. Monsieur stood by me, looking on. 'Remember everything I taught you, Jeanne' he said, handing me the Brown Bess, primed. 'You keep a candle lit, to warn you against any unwarranted approach. You point this in their faces, tell them you will shoot. In the meantime, I shall work to overturn this scandalous affront.'

I did not speak, but roused myself, and shoved my few belongings in a duffel sack, and trooped below obediently to find the purser.

The ship, as luck would have it, was at that time in that stretch of southern waters called the Doldrums. My position on the gun deck as things turned out was not too exposed – a hammock slung between two rafters near a sailmaker who spoke little but who grew protective of me and kept much unwonted curiosity away.

I soon grew less afraid: Vivès' fascination with me seemed to ebb in counterpoint to the degree of mercury's rise. The world was somnolent, inert, and dulled. I slept untroubled for a period of fifteen nights. The windless tropics made our progress slow. Monsieur went off the deck each day to rest his leg, inflamed once more by heat.

I worked alone in the cool darkness of the hold, my head dulled by the vapours of preserving spirit, and was storing some new soft-bodied mollusks, when a shadow moving past the grating startled me.

Vivès stepped out of the shadows, grabbed me, wrenched my arm behind my back. He doubled me forward over a waist-high coil of rope. I felt his filthy crotch grind hard against my rear, the rasp of stubble close behind my ear. 'Don't think you fool me, you bitch.' The stench of brandy on his breath. 'I know we need to take a closer look at this.'

His filthy hand was in my pantaloon. But I threw my head back and struck his nose. His hands rose to the pain and in this instant, I span loose, I raised my Brown Bess, cocked, and primed. 'Step back,' I said. 'Or I will shoot.'

He took a single step towards me, then I fired.

Tahiti

THENCEFORTH HE DIDN'T trouble me again. Vivès lay suppurating in the dark, half of his face and his mind gone too. The incident was called an accident, no charges pressed. Without the surgeon's pressure, Captain Bougainville agreed that I could move back to my former berth.

And then, a little after six o'clock on 12th, June 1769, we spied a native village standing a half dozen leagues off to the East. Under a line of shady palms above a curl of yellow beach, a cluster of grass houses stood packed around a clearing fire, emitting plumes of greenish smoke.

Monsieur stood on the foredeck training a glass on the scene. He passed it to me, and I saw a crowd of people frenzied like a tribe of ants whose nest has just been prodded with a stick. They went racing down the beach to boats, and began loading them with fruit and flowers, feathered fowl and squealing hogs, bolts of cloth and flower garlands, rushing to the water's edge and rowing out like Harridans across the bay. A hullabaloo blew up all around, bedecked with flowers, the same bright flowers we saw for the first time upon the atolls ten leagues east, that we had called Bougainvillea, in the captain's honour, the boats came out towards us through the surf.

My eye was drawn at first to women: women with their long hair loose over their breasts, garlands of white flowers around their necks, braids of green leaves on their heads. Their dark skin luminous with oil.

As they came close to the ship's side, the frenzied rhythm of the drums became more deafening. My heart was beating faster as the first prow struck the ship. A boy leapt like a cat from his canoe; missing the ropes he fell back to the sea. The women's laughter rang loud in the din as he swam fluently toward a second cable tossed by men who dangled out to help him up over the ship's rails onto the deck.

Hogs and roosters rose hand over hand. Platters of green fruit, fresh, and plentiful. The women climbed the ladders, leapt the rails, hung garlands of flowers about the seamen's' necks, their laughter ringing as they met.

Vahine

ONE MAN PRESSED so close to me that I could smell the sweat of his bare arms and chest, the oil in his hair, see the detail of the mantras on his skin, etched in ink as black as molasses. He made a low sound in his throat, pointing first to my chest, then his own.

'Vahine.'

I showed him a trinket. A flash of bright light glinted on his face. Like a man in a wig shop, he gazed at his reflection. He smiled and turned his head to catch the angles. He stooped a little to facilitate the view. He held his head to one side, grinning foolishly.

Again, he straightened, pointing to himself, to me. 'Vahine.'

The heat was fierce and sweat ran down my back in rivulets of damp. He obliged me to raise my arms, then touched my hipbones, pinched my waist, ran his two hands along the contours of my flanks.

'Perhaps,' Monsieur said, appearing at my shoulder, 'We should fall back now. He seems rather intent on your attention, Jeanne.'

Inquisitive, the man shoved close.

Monsieur removed his hat, lowered it with care onto the boy's head. The boy snatched it away, wheeled it off through the air, out of the circle, over the side, so it landed in the ocean some distance away.

He shoved Monsieur aside, out of his way. 'Vahine,' he said. He mimed the shape of breasts, of hips. 'Vahine,' he said, looking around for approval. Pointing at his chest then at mine.

And all the time, behind me, smirking in his garlands with a girl on his arm, Vivés stood with rat's eyes looking on.

Tattoo

THE PEOPLE OF that island had a method whereby they draw ink out of a nut which they have previously burnt. They dip a sharp point made of bone into a bowl of oil and hammer it into the skin. This action draws serum and a little surface blood. When they are done, they wash the marks and bind the spot in a poultice of leaves and herbs.

Some days later, inscribed in flesh, remains the mark, the mantra – whichever portrait they conspire.

They call this work *tattoo*.

At noon and once again at evening, the men and women go together to the river to wash. They are exceedingly cleanly.

The women wrap their torsos in bark cloth, but let it fall around their waists at sunset, adopting an easy kind of undress. They wear bonnets of cocoa leaves, entwined with flowers, their only jewellry a hoop of fashioned coral in one ear. They knot their hair in plaits (*tamou*) and anoint their hair with oil (*monoe.*) The oil is made of coconut infused with aloe balm. It is a pungent mix, but infinitely preferable to the odiferous stink of European toes and armpits. Their houses are made of palm thatch laid on poles with mats beneath.

They eat under the shade of nearby trees.

They couple openly, delight in bawdy humour, have scant regard for European notions of propriety.

They knew me as a woman straightaway.

They inked my name upon my flesh: *Baret*.

Unmasked

THE CAPTAIN, REALISING Monsieur's fraud, said he was compromised and could not in all conscience take us home. So, he would set us off at Suva on the return trip. Suva, in the Sumatra Islands, where we could wait discreetly for some other ship, perhaps a year might be discreet, before we could return to France. No mention would be made in any log of M. Commerson's servant having been aboard the Etoile or the Boudeuse, of her origin, or the circumstances of her unveiling. Silence would be maintained by all aboard, even Surgeon Vivès, who had given Captain Bougainville his oath.

'All shall remain silent on the subject of your female servant, sir, so silent it shall be as if she never lived.'

Ahuturo, the islander who first knew me – who recognised me as a woman when a hundred and one Frenchman had been fooled – even he was sworn to secrecy, on the condition of his passage back to Europe.

Two weeks later we were on the quayside at Suva, prepared to look for lodgings in that town.

Mauritius, one year later

SOME SIX MONTHS later, tired of Suva, we took ship to Mauritius, came here aboard a French whaler, our passage paid for by Monsieur. Our days passed pleasantly enough, one after the next, but trade in this place is much better, and Monsieur has some society.

Most days I sit at my table with a view of the bay, lighting my candle as the slow day fades, filling these pages with my recollections.

Monsieur is there below me in the port, trading silks for spices, timber for molasses; exchanging pleasantries with those few sailors from the European ships who pause here and traverse those slumbering docks. I trust him, you might say.

Though for myself I keep my hair cut close and wear men's trousers too, a smock to cover my loose breasts, unbound so I can breathe as I lean forward here to write. Each day I find myself a little further from my work, as my ripe belly swells. The rainy season will come soon and then my child will come into the world, and I will go out less, stay more often in my garden, tending to my plants, wandering perhaps with Monsieur in the darkness on the white sands in the moonlight, with our new baby slung across my hip.

But this is where I live, where I belong, reflecting now on who I was, who I became, unfixed – like days and nights, we shuttle back and forth along a scale, through sunrise to sunset, through different phases in our lives, shading out of one condition to the next.

But here, on this small island, now, waiting for my little loaf to rise, I hope I have found peace at last.

Ceiling

Hannah Sutherland

Limitless

WE'RE IN THE car but we don't know where we're going.

You slide your forefinger down the condensation on the car window and draw a Very Sad Face then swipe it across with your palm. I close my eyes and pray (even though none of us is religious but maybe we should be) because Nee, he's taking his hands off the steering wheel, losing control, then gaining it just as a car comes speeding towards us. It feels like when we're inflating balloons before a birthday party, filling them with air, being cocky wee shites, chancing our luck as they grow and grow then right before the P-O-P, we just stop blowing and the balloon deflates. It's exactly like that, only without the birthday cake.

'Och, ye pair are so feckin' boring,' Da goes, which is a blatant lie because you're definitely not. I don't think I'm boring either. I'm eleven and eleven-year-olds are never boring, so Miss Cox says. She says we are *the future*, and there's no such thing as 'reaching our potential' because there's no ceiling to our learning. Our potential is limitless.

She tells us to imagine ourselves as wee seeds, buried deep in soil, and with all this learning she keeps giving us, we grow and grow and grow through the ceiling, bustin' our potential. 'You can do anything!' she exclaims from the front of class with her hands extended to us like she's grasping at the imaginary stems and willing them up to the sky, tears in her eyes, looking like she just fuckin' loves us all, like we're these magnificent beings who can do absolutely anything.

Ach, funny auld Miss Cox. The dreamer.

Limited

KERRY KEEPS HIS woollen jumper in a Tesco bag at the back of the wardrobe. She wears it to bed sometimes when she wants to feel close to him. It scratches her skin and brings it out blotchy. She doesn't seem to care.

Wall

DA DRIVES US to the harbour, tells me he wants to show me a trick. Says to close my eyes; I'm a bird. Not like the seagull who stole my sandwich that time outside Bonbons. Remember, I screamed, and you swore, but the fecker took my sandwich all the same. It's all right though cause the cheese spread was at least a week out of date; saved me from a dose of the shits.

Nah, I'm not like that kind of bird at all. I'm graceful like the ones Miss Cox tells us about in closed comprehension, swooping and diving, and I've got golden feathers, and I'm properly soaring over the sea and the air's whacking me in the face like a slap, but sure, I don't care because I'm free and… oh Christ. That's a bit high.

'Da!' I shout. 'Put me down!'

Some lad's knocked clumps out of Da down the local. His eye's folded over and it's all the colours of the rainbow already.

I'm laughing a wee bit, cause it's quite funny being flung but then he drops me further, dangles my legs over the pier edge above the waves, dark, unforgiving waves.

'Da!' I say again. I'm not feeling much like a bird now.

I hold my breath and try not to scream; scream and he'll do it more, scream and he'll enjoy it. Then you – braver, bolder, fearless you – just roll your eyes and tell him to 'quit it' – as though it really is that easy.

'Ma will be fumin, ye know, *Jim*' you say, arms folded, tapping your fingers.

It's not until you pull on his arm and go, 'Enough now,' that he takes heed. He laughs and puts me on the concrete; the lights on my trainers flash bright like little warning signs nobody notices.

He picks you up next, only this time he hangs you lower. Drops catches, catches drops, and I'm sorry, I can't help it. I'm screaming. 'Stop it, Da! Oh please, oh please.'

You remain silent, tossed against the rising sun. A ragdoll.

When Da's bored of flinging you about on the pier, he puts you back on the cement and you shove him so hard I think he's going over the edge, but you're not that strong and he barely moves.

'I'm only messin'.' Da says.

You scowl, turn and walk towards the carpark behind the harbour wall. I scurry behind you 'cause for a moment, Da has that unpredictable look in his eye, like a feral dog sizing its victim, and I'm not in the mood for another dangle before breakfast.

Christ, can't think of anything worse on an empty tummy.

Air

KERRY PLAYS HARD to get, in the beginning, with Jim, until he wears her down. Turns up at her Mammy and Da's house with supermarket flowers and own brand chocolate and stuffed teddies he nicked from his toddler nephew to impress; it works. She's not use to such attention. She's clean swept off her feet by this older man with freckles and dimples and hair as wild as fire. He takes her dancing. Spins her around until her feet don't touch the ground and her golden hair flows like it's part of the air and she's flying.

'Ach, I'm off soon. Uni,' she goes when he asks her to be his girlfriend, not just the lass he sneaks down to the harbour with to learn how to undo a girls bra in the dark.

A gull plays in the water, splashes like it belongs to the sea.

'So?' he goes. 'Do lassies no have boyfriends at uni like?'

'Some do. But no those who don't want to be tied down. I might be away to meet the love of my life, ye never know.'

She's joking. Sort of.

He sulks then. Takes his hand off her tit, slumps, inhales the sea and the salt and scowls at the cool blue below.

House

WHEN WE GET home from the pier, Mammy's pacing at the front door. Her mouth is in a thin, cracked line and her skin's blotchy with tears, and she's saying, 'For Christs sake, Jim, what are ye playing at?' and he's saying, 'Sure, am I not allowed to take me own girls to see the sunrise?'

She slaps him, hard, across his face, a loud smack, then pushes his chest, says, 'No! Ye can't just sneak into my house and take them without telling me.'

We just stand there. I hold your hand because it's just what we do when they get going. You give it a wee squeeze.

Da lets out a loud sigh and throws his hands in the air. 'Fine. Fine. Ye bloody win, as always,' and then he turns to us. 'Gee yer auld man a kiss then.'

I do it because even though he's an arse ninety percent of the time, he's still Da, but you shake your head, turn away – older, cooler, stubborn – and this makes him wild. He clutches your cheeks between his mucky hands like you're food.

Mammy's shouting, 'Jim, she doesn't want to. Leave

her be! Ye can't force her.'

I give you a look, scrunch up my forehead, and beg, tell you, *just do it Nee, please. For me.* You catch it. Your shoulders sag, defeated, and you turn to him, say, 'Fine.'

You kiss his cheek.

'That wasn't so hard was it, Nee?' he says, wiping snot from his nose with the back of his hand. You just shrug, walk past our rusty bicycles, without looking back. They look lonely, left together to rot against the wall.

'Bye then, Da,' I say, and follow you into the house.

'I'll get that DVD ye wanna watch,' he calls after me. 'I'll get it. Promise.'

You're in our room, your fingers down your throat, bringing up nothing into the bin you keep beside your bed.

'I must have messed up,' you say.

Your phone starts singing with Justin Bieber, and you glance at it, but carry on, get back to whatever it is you feel you need to do. I answer for you, and it's your boyfriend Ross and he talks away about football for the twenty-three minutes you are busy, and although I know nothing about Celtic, I listen all the same. What else is there to do?

Blind

KERRY PRETENDS SHE doesn't know that Nee blames herself for Jim's early morning snatch to the harbour. She ignores the noise coming from Nee's room when she's hard at work, punishing herself. Kerry gets the wine instead, pours a satisfying glass. Drinks it like its juice until her head is fuzzy and she can pretend everything's normal.

Kerry knows Nee always blames herself when Jim misbehaves.

Roots

I'M TEN. MAMMY kicks Da out for good when he's caught fingering Easy Sheila from two doors down. I don't even know what that means but Mammy says it with her face all screwed up like she's sucked lemons for days. Da lives with Easy Sheila for about five days until she kicks him out too, cause he pisses all over her fabric sofa which is tricky, really, getting rid of the smell and stains. Bet Easy Sheila wishes she'd gone for fake leather now. You'd just wipe that mess right off, no hassle.

Da did that on our sofa all the time after a sesh, especially when the footie was on telly. Mammy was always out with the Febreze and bleach. Should have got shares in the stuff, she would joke, spraying and scrubbing till her fingers bled and her knees burned raw.

Now Da kips on our Uncle Mike's sofa or in the bed of whoever he's sweet on after a night down the local. Your boyfriend, Ross, says Da's always blind drunk and cursin', up to no good, with his half chewed up forefinger pressed to the barman's chest, demanding more.

'Ach fecks sake. I'll have another if I want,' he goes,

and Ross says nobody wants to sit next to him, stinkin' of piss and booze and desperation.

Ross's wise, for a seventeen-year-old. He's bold too, sneaking into pubs and the like when he's underage, but he's built like a tree and so he fits right in. Keeps you rooted Nee. Keeps you safe.

Missing

KERRY SITS ON the floor when he's gone. She listens as the landline rings on and on, the people who can afford cars toot their horns and the gulls cry out for food. She wants to feel guilty for letting them starve, but she's gone all numb inside instead.

Unspoken rules

IN THE PLAYGROUND, the other girls are talking about periods and who has them in our year and who hasn't and boys and who we will take to the disco at the Tattie Sheds on Friday night. All I'm thinking about is how Mammy forgot to make me a packed lunch and how I'll have to beg to share Lyn's and her Mammy always makes ham sandwiches and I'm trying to be a vegetarian. Hunger or the animals. My tummies like a storm already and it's only feckin break time.

'Yours haven't started yet, have they?' Lyn says, pulling me from my thoughts of a poor pig in a slaughterhouse. You made me watch the video, Nee, remember? You made me and Ross and Mammy and Da watch it, and I cried, and Ross went pale and Mammy lit up a cigarette and Da put some bacon in the frying pan.

'Nah. No yet,' I say.

'You're the only one in our group not to have started them,' she says, as though periods are a thing I can control. 'And you haven't started shaving your legs yet either.'

'Aye? Oh well,' I say, folding my arms across my chest. Lyn's started wearing a bra too, but she's got no tits yet, so she stuffs it with balled together socks, the eejit. 'Our Nee says periods are sore and I'm lucky. Nee says I'll hate them for the rest of my life until I go through the manopause so what's the hurry to get started.'

'Menopause.'

'That's what I said.'

Lyn wrinkles her nose. 'Who are ye takin' to the Tattie Sheds then?'

'No one,' I say. 'I'm just gonna take myself.'

The other girls snigger. Obviously, I've said the wrong thing, as *always*, because sure, I must have been absent the day the manual to Being Very Popular was given out.

'Ye can't go *yerself*,' Lyn says. 'Ye have to go with a boy.'

'Right so,' I say.

I peer around at the dateless boys in our year but none of them are appealing, Nee, because there's Spotty Frank in the corner picking his nose and devouring its goods, and Wee Johnny next to him with his hands down his actual boxers giving his tiny dick a fiddle – we all saw it at P.E last month when he sat on the grass, and he was bold as fuckin brass, with his legs open wide, cock and bollix just *there*, the wind blowing the material sideways, Miss Cox beaming red like the traffic lights none of us pay attention to, and Wee Johnny, ignoring the North Sea breeze.

Then there's Harry or Larry with the glasses stuck back together with masking tape down the middle because Lanky Craig stood on them by mistake in P.E but he got a detention anyway because Harry slash Larry said Lanky Craig did it On Purpose, which I know for sure he didn't, because Lanky Craig is harmless.

Spoiled for choice, me.

Awake

I'M TUGGING NEE through the stalls lining the usually serene town centre, palms slick with perspiration. There are stalls selling the fish the locals have caught and people have come to the town from neighbouring villages, all desperate for the freshest catch.

'Nee will ye just keep a hold of Mammy's hand.'

Just then, Nee slips my hand and takes off through the crowds.

I'm a bleedin' eejit. In what world should I have taken my unpredictable two-and-a-half-year-old to a feckin' Seafood Festival on the hottest day of the year so far when I've had a grand total of three hours' sleep. Will I ever sleep again?

'Nee! Och, Nee, will ye stop!'

Nee's quick on her feet – being slight and two feet tall. I hold onto my bump which is quickly filling my c-section pouch with one hand and my newly heavy tits with the other and make a mental note to purchase a bra that offers better support.

Nee slips and falls into the side of a stall, pulls on the

cloth to steady herself and takes a bed of cold ice and half a dozen mackerel onto the cement with her.

Ach shite.

A vein in my neck pulses as a heat travels from my belly to my face as I hug her.

'Leg hurts, Mammy.'

I look up at the red faced, greasy stall holder and say, 'I'm so sorry for all of this. She's been on one all day…'

'You'll have to pay for these,' the man says, crossing his arms. 'What a bleedin' waste…'

'Oh, yeah. Of course,' I say, pulling the backpack and placing it in front of me as I fiddle through nappies and changes of clothing and endless snacks until I find my purse. 'It was an accident. I'm so sorry…'

And just as I hand the man a note, which I've already spent in my head on a more supportive bra, Nee wriggles away, grabs a mackerel between her wee palms and runs.

'Bloody *hell*. Nee!'

'Shouldn't have kids if ye can't control them…'

'Nee!' I call, scanning the streets for cars but sure, in one small blessing, the roads are blocked off for the market.

Nee stops beside a fisherman with broad shoulders and before I can reach her, she drops the mackerel in the coffee cup he's holding. Christ.

'Mine!' I call from behind him, panting, doubled over. 'She's mine.'

'Oh! Hello, Mammy!' Nee exclaims, like it's a complete coincidence that I am here, chasing after her, sweating out of every pore of my body.

And then the man turns his head towards me and the skin around his eyes crinkles as he smiles.

'Ye owe me a coffee,' he says, motioning to the fish poking out of his cup, then he eyes my growing belly, and his face turns to concern. 'I'm Ewan. C'mon. Let me help get ye home.'

Daisy Chains

LANKY CRAIG MARRIED me when we were eight, actually. I spent the whole feckin lunch time outside making a daisy chain to go around my head then married him with a bunch of dandelions that made his face glow golden in one hand, and he shoved a Hula Hoop on the ring finger of my other hand, kissed me cheek and everyone went 'Ooo' with their hands under their chins and their fingers pointing down the way. We felt really grown up for a whole eleven minutes before the bell rang and we had to get back to all the learning.

Lanky Craig wasn't so good with 'exclusivity', you call it, because he married half the class and the year below me within the next week. What can you do? At least my ring was edible.

I look over at the lads and sigh.

Ach, he'll do.

I leave the gaggle of giggling girls behind me and walk over to the lads. I peer up at Lanky Craig who looks down at me and turns red, like those tomatoes Mammy says we've to eat with our supper, but you smuggle them up your sleeves and flush them down the loo. You say they're boggin' things, ye can't stand the fuckers.

'Ye got a date for the Sheds then, Craig?' I ask, putting my hands on my hips like I'm cool and ask lanky lads out all the time. He shakes his head. 'Wanna come with me?'

He shrugs, goes, 'Sure.'

I walk back to the girls and tell them he's coming with me, like it's no big deal but my hands are shaking, and my knees knock together like an out of time drum. Sure, this growing up thing and all its rules is bustin' up my head.

Home

THERE'S A STORM raging outside and a pot of tea brewing inside. Jim's boat is moored in the harbour. The wooden fence surrounding the house is away to go and the rain is battering against the windows. Kerry's sitting on Ewan's sofa feeding her new-born girl as Nee flicks through 'A House is a House for Me'. The flames hug the logs inside the fireplace. The waves outside scream at the harbour walls and Kerry feels smug and content that her family are cosy. Ewan's taken fresh scones from the oven and he's slicing strawberries to go with the cream.

'A wee treat,' he says, and Kerry thinks that yes, life with Ewan in it is just that. A treat.

The door knocks then, and Jim comes tumbling in, bringing the storm with him. He stops in the middle of the living room, sways slightly, refocusing his glassy eyes. 'This looks cosy.'

'It is very cosy in here,' Kerry says. 'Yes.'

Jim looks from her to Ewan and then at his girls. 'C'mon then. Let's head home.'

'But it's wild out there,' Ewan says, hugging his woollen jumper to his chest.

Jim looks at him and Ewan shrinks before him, head to shoulders, all scrunched down together.

The baby wails on the walk home as Kerry holds her to her chest, trying to keep in some of the warmth from Ewan's home. Jim pulls Nee along as the wind blows her sideways. Her fingers are slippery and although they only live ten minutes away, they're all soaked through.

Kerry towels Nee's hair, changes her into her pyjamas, sends her to bed with her hands over her ears so she can't hear Jim roar.

Sure, the storm drowns him out anyway. Almost.

Slipping Through Her Fingers

THE NIGHT OF the Tattie Sheds, you paint my eyes with kohl and spray my wrists with the perfume you stole from Semi Chem.

'It only costs a few pounds,' you said when you came home with a bag full. 'So, it's not like I've feckin robbed a bank, Miss Moral.'

I'm glad you nicked it; my wrists smell nice.

You've skipped your throwing up to help get me ready. You're fighting the urge to start but sure, you don't. You stay put and keep on making me look older than I am.

'There. Ye look pretty,' you say. 'But no pulling that Lanky Craig. You've the rest of your life to neck lads. Just go and enjoy the dancin'.'

'Ach sure, you were neckin' lads when you were younger than me.'

'Cheeky shite.'

Mammy takes some photos on her disposable camera of me, next to the mantlepiece.

'Christ, my wee girl is all grown up.'

'Mammy, that's the point,' Nee grins.

Mammy says nothing more, just stands clutching that camera like its gold and then she sits down for a long while as though my growing up has happened suddenly instead of right before her eyes.

Happy

THEY'RE AT A wedding dance, and Jim is bleezin' at the bar. Kerry and Ewan and the girls dance on the shiny wooden floor together. Ewan's fishing boat isn't out this weekend and he's grateful to be there, with them all. Kerry's in bare feet because her heels are buggered with blisters from cheap shite shoes, the girls sliding about like the floor is made of ice, their tights filthy with dirt and picked at the bottom. The function room isn't known from its attention to cleanliness.

Nee laughs as Ewan flings her sister around like a feather and Kerry moves her hips and punches the air with her fists. They scream the words to the songs into each other's faces and then they're jumping, nearly touching the roof, shifting that ceiling until they're grabbing the stars.

'Christ, I love ye,' Ewan shouts to Kerry who doesn't care who hears. Sure, Jim's so pissed he won't remember it in the morning anyway.

They dance for hours and hours like they're just one person, all wrapped up together in fancy dresses and

sweaty limbs, and they are happy.
    Really very happy.

Tattie Sheds

YOU AND ROSS walk me to the Sheds. Ross's legs are long and I've to run to keep up with the pair of ye, my pumps slamming the concrete as we walk.

'Smoke?' Ross says, handing me his lit one.

'Ta,' I say, inhaling like a movie star but it makes me cough. I think, probably, lungs aren't developed for smoking when you're eleven but maybe, when I'm thirteen they will be, and I'll be more successful. Sure, I can wait. Got the rest of my life.

Lanky Craig's leaning against the steel of the shed when we walk up to him. He's wearing a smart tartan shirt and it's tucked into his skinny jeans which make his legs look like two long poles. He's put something in his hair that makes it look greasy and he's shaved his smooth face, cut it along his jaw and he looks edgy. He's not even started puberty yet.

Neither have I, which is deeply sad given how I can't join in when the other girls help each other out when they've forgotten to take tampons to school or they're sharing razors in the loos to get rid of their leg hair. I talk to my legs all the time and tell my dark hair to sprout but they just don't feckin' listen.

'You look good,' Lanky Craig says. A boy of deep compliments.

'Nice shirt,' Ross says to Lanky Craig. 'Very Scottish.'

'I am Scottish,' Lanky Craig goes.

'I'm Scottish too,' I go, common ground.

'I know,' Lanky Craig says.

'Christ.' You roll your eyes. 'Now we've established everyone at this feckin' disco is Scottish, given that we live in bloody Scotland, can ye go and enjoy yourselves?'

I grin at you. It's the same grin that Ross gives you, cause he loves you too.

'Bye Nee, bye Ross,' I say.

I grab Lanky Craig's hand and lead him into the Tattie Sheds which has been decorated with some rainbow-coloured bunting and flashing lights. The term 'shed' itself is deceiving because it's more like a barn and is made of steel instead of wood like the shed in our backie. Big in size, big enough for about sixty of us to dance, eighty to be crammed, one hundred to be extremely uncomfortable and squashed, one hundred and fifty for the shed to come crumbling down. In October, they store tatties in here during the Tattie holidays when some of the lads get roped into helping with the pickin' and we get two weeks off school to bum around doing nothin' which is better than doing somethin' at school.

Heirloom

JIM'S FURIOUS WITH Kerry, says, 'He'll never replace me,' and she goes, 'Good. Who'd want to replace *you* anyway,' but this makes him mad, makes him seethe, turns him to the booze and the shots and the white lines.

Trashes the house, breaks her late Granny's posh China, breaks her arm too.

'Not in front of the girls,' she says through gritted teeth. 'Christ, do what ye bleedin' want to me, but not in front of the girls.'

Ewan holds Kerry at night, his calloused fingers entwined with hers, and she tries to be strong, but with Ewan, she doesn't need to do that anymore.

Outside But In

I SPOT LYN and 'the gang' by the soft drinks stand which Miss Cox is standing by with a t-shirt on it saying something about missing the moon and landing in the stars. Ah, good auld Miss Cox. Loves an inspirational quote.

The five girls are standing together, and their five dates are huddled together, and I wonder why there's such insistence on 'bringing a date' and how unfair it would have been, for me to have excluded from the primary seven disco based on Lanky Craig saying *no*.

I wave but they don't really look at me, until Lyn goes: 'Oh, what's that awful smell?' and the girls laugh, and I think of my wrists and how proud I was to wear your lovely stolen perfume.

'Tatties?' I say, all they all laugh like I'm funny and walk to the dancefloor. The boys follow them, even Lanky Craig.

I hope you're having more fun than I am, Nee. I hope you're neckin' Ross and he's doing that thing with his fingers up your skirt that ye like. You don't know that I know he does that to ye. But I saw ye once, behind the bikes in the park when I was meant to be playing but Lyn and the girls said I couldn't play, *again,* and so I wandered off.

'Are you having lots of fun?' Miss Cox asks me.

'Sure,' I say. I wish my dress had pockets because I really want to shove my hands into something because I don't know what to do with them but my dress is flat down the sides and so I cuddle my body instead.

'You should go and dance with your friends,' Miss Cox says.

She has eyes and ears that work. She surely knows they're not my friends, that I just tag along with them cause if I didn't, I'd be alone, and it's better to be with people who don't like you than be by yourself, Da says, and he should know.

'Ach nah,' I say. My arms are wrapped around my body now and I can touch my spine. I'm like one of those double-jointed people whose limbs can bend and stretch into weird lookin' positions that make your head funny, wondering how they do that. 'I'm not into dancin'.'

Miss Cox blinks a few times. 'Grand. Grand.'

Heavy

KERRY HOLDS EWAN'S jumper to her cheeks, inhales his scent of tobacco and salt and fish and lets the wool irritate and suffocate her. Sure, her belly's full of ice and her chest hurts when she breathes anyway.

She fills her nose up with the smell of him, but he's already gone.

Different

THE MUSIC IS making my ears bleed it's so loud. I nod my head along to the beat and pretend I know what song is playing but I don't. Lyn knows the song. She belts out the words and moves her arms above her head and grinds her body into Lanky Craig, and then she's kissing him.

Oh.

And I mean I DO NOT even *care* about Lanky Craig, but they all turn to look at me and sure, I've started crying anyway. I'm not even *sad*.

It's like that time in class, when I read out a story that I'd written all about Ewan and my eyes just filled up like a sink whose plug's been whipped away and down came the tears, for no reason at all. And I just carried on reading, cause sure, what else could I have done? The whole class looked at me like I was a rare species in a specific museum that only housed my kind, and then Miss Cox kept me back after class and gave me a hug which I know she's not meant to do, being a teacher. She held me to her chest and stroked my hair and told me everything was going to be okay and if I ever, *ever* needed to talk to her, I could.

That was kind of auld Miss Cox, but it made me cry again.

Lost at Sea

KERRY GOES TO the sea to breathe. It's winter and the houses along the sea front have their tinselled trees in the windows, their wreaths on the door. Her head is sore, and her chest is thick, and she has no idea how to get home.

Oh Da Oh Da Oh Da

I'M IN THE Tattie Sheds and they're all gawping, and I don't want to be here anymore, so I run to the toilets.

I go to the sink and I scrub my wrists with the cheap unscented soap from the white dispensers and I rub, scrub, erase, until I smell of nothing at all. I close my eyes and tell you to come and get me, telepathically sending you a message. I scrunch them up real tight but when I open them, you're not there and my eyes are black from the kohl.

There's a group gathered in the centre of the dance-floor when I leave the loos. I think it's probably still Lyn and Lanky Craig kissing and they're putting on an excellent show and I hear them go: 'She's comin'! She's back.' I head for the exit, towards you and Ross, where you'll be sitting sharing a bottle of cider and a cigarette, waiting for me, but then I see you, in the middle of the crowd, and Ross, with a figure hanging from his tree-like frame, and, oh this is *not* happening.

It's only Da.

Da's crashed the party. Da has crashed the Tattie

Shed party for eleven-year-olds. The bleedin' numpty.

You're bright red. You're trying to steady him but he's cursin' and shoutin' and looking for me. 'Go home, Da,' you say. You'll be blamin' yourself for all of this.

'Ach, there ye are,' he goes and tugs my hand. 'I've got that film ye wanted. Borrowed it from Uncle Mike. C'mon, we can go watch it.'

'Da,' I say, quietly. 'I'm at the disco.'

He looks around for the first time, it seems. The group's all staring at him, and Miss Cox has her hands closed together over her chest and her eyes are so wide. I think she's saying a prayer for me.

'Och, Christ, so ye are,' Da goes, gulping down some beer from the can he keeps swinging around. Someone should be following him around with a cup; it'd be full in no time at all. 'So, ye comin'?'

I look over at Lanky Craig who has Lyn's lipstick on his chin, and he looks at his shoes, which are shite supermarket own brands. Lyn grins at me, her wicked eyes gleaming. Sure, she'll enjoy talking about this on Monday, and I'll smile and accept it all the same.

'Yeah, I'm coming Da,' I say, taking his hand.

I lead him out the Shed and he follows, burpin' and drinking and laughing like we're normal.

'Fuckin disgrace,' you say, pushing his back when we get out. 'Mammy's going to kill ye. Ach, Da. Ye bleedin' spoil everything.'

Goodbye

THE SEA IS completely calm when Kerry gets the call. There's not even a breeze. She thinks it's a joke and so she laughs. Thinks it's one of Jim's mates down the local being cruel.

'Please stop laughing.'

'Och, is this you Sheila? Is Jim at ye again? Jaysus. That's a good one. Ye got me there, for a second. Bloody hell, the lot o' ye are sick. Sick. Leave me the fuck alone.'

It's when the phone rings again and again and again that she realises her hands are shaking.

It has to be a joke. Christ, please, please, let it be a joke.

Normal

WHEN WE'RE OUTSIDE the house, Da walks right past the front door, stumbles and trips his way away from us.

'Da?' I shout. 'Da? We not watching that movie, Da? No?'

'Ach,' he goes. 'Another time, lass.' He throws me the DVD, but it lands a few inches from my feet. The case opens and the DVD springs from its place onto the ground. 'I'm gonna go head back to the pub, see what's the crack. See yi the morn.'

'Right,' I say. 'Right, okay.' But he's already halfway down the street.

'I'll go after him,' Ross says. 'Make sure he doesn't get himself fuckin killed.'

'Get to fuck, Da,' you shout, but sure, he must have wax in his ears, cause he doesn't turn around.

Entwined

JIM FINDS KERRY by the beach. Her nose is red, and her toes are frozen solid, and she doesn't care at all. It's dark. They can barely see the water. Can only hear it, whispering in the night, telling secrets but nobody is listening.

Jim sniffs, coughs, sips on some water. 'Ach. I fucked right up, Kerry.'

She cocks her head to him and wrinkles her brow. 'With what specifically?'

'Tonight. I really, really fucked up.'

She glances behind her to Ross, leaning against the brick wall, smoking, looking awkwardly in their direction. He gives Kerry a wee wave then looks down at his scuffed trainers.

'Oh Christ, what did ye do?'

He shakes his head. She takes her hand in his, leans her head on his shoulder.

'I don't deserve them girls.'

She sighs. 'No. Ye don't. But you're the only Da they've got so.'

He sniffs again. Spits phlegm on the sand. 'Poor fuckers.'

Kerry feels something inside her snap and the world comes back into focus. She was fading away only an hour ago, loosing herself to the air. She's surprised all her limbs are still there. That she is a living, breathing thing rather than a shell. She blinks several times and allows herself to cry. Everything aches. Her chest, her back, her heart.

'I miss him, Jim. I really miss him'

'I know.'

They sit there, for a while longer and try to make each other better by saying nothing else at all.

Ceiling

IN OUR ROOM, you stick your fingers down your throat, Nee. You heave and spew and poke your tonsils, heave and spew, then you repeat. Binge on more snacks. Repeat.

'Nee?' I say, now in my pyjamas. 'Nee, can you stop that?'

'In a minute,' you say, but it's already been thirty-three. 'I must have messed up this morning. Christ, I'm so sorry. I'm so sorry.'

'Nee… please stop.'

'It's all my fault,' you go, but it's not Nee. None of it is. It never is. It's all on Da. He means well, he's good deep down, but the good's real deep now, buried under years of booze and drugs and trouble. But it's never you, Nee. Not ever.

I climb into my bed and lie in the pale, blue dark, listening to you strain.

It's only when I start to sob, that you creep in beside me.

'Ach, I'm sorry,' you say. 'I'm just so angry.'

You wrap your arms around me. They're small – like

your waist, your chest, your hips – a little person. But although your body is tiny, your love for me is infinite, vast, endless. You nuzzle your nose into my hair and just hold me.

The ceiling above us crumbles and our roots, forever intertwined, unravel and grow, bustin' on through. We can be anything, Nee. Do anything when we're holdin' each other like this. I close my eyes and I'm so close to falling sleep, where everything's calmer.

And then you get out of my bed.

Bleedin' start all over again.

The Girl Who Survived

Dawn Siofra North

Part One

Casting Off

ON MY FIRST night aboard as we lost sight of land, she told me the rule: I'm to let go of you too.

You, the girl I was, back when I believed I knew certainty. Here, I depend completely on my elderly guide: for the fire that she keeps (never scorching the deck), and the guidance she gathers from consulting with seabirds.

I have so many questions, but I keep them stuffed down, beneath a pretence of composure.

Will she see my lack of confidence, if I want to know
am I safe?
is this hope?
who am I, now?

Seeking

THIS CAN'T BE right.

When I took the job here, it seemed just right. I'd thought it so elegant: the moulded ceiling like empty wedding-dress boxes, showing their pink insides. It felt like the perfect place to hide; I've always wrapped myself up in stories. And who even uses the library these days? Just people like me who actually like the smell of rotting pages.

Except that now, *she* comes every Thursday.

The first time, she'd announced herself into the gloom that stretched between afternoon tea-break and closing. Hair an explosion of corkscrew curls – but controlled, like the soft eruption of champagne. Spike heels made echo-less by the carpet tiles that cover the old ceramic ones. In her left hand, she held one of those swipey new phones that give you the whole of the internet; in the other, her borrower card, number -994.

The titles she reserves (for collection each week) are the last ones I'd select for someone like her: long-buried tales of factories and flooding, dug up from the deep storage of the library basement.

Between her visits, to kill time when things go dead, I sneak into her books before she comes to pick them up. With most of it, I can see the appeal. Flood mythology, dramatic tales, stories of survival and renewal. But some of it's baffling, like the little book listing household items from an era of hardship long since left behind.

Today is Friday. She hasn't been yet and we close in five minutes. Stupidly, my throat is tight with unswallowed loss. I don't want to spend the weekend wondering if she'd got what she came for and she's never coming back. Outside, the cold white sky is giving way to dusk and the ceiling lights laugh at me, their reflections jeering in the darkening windows. Choking down my frustration, I'm in no mood to help when I feel someone else approach the desk.

This really can't be right.

He's holding the card for borrower -994, his eyes flashing blue, hair a wild mess of brown curls. The desk is a shield, but I still feel displayed and exposed when he says, 'Hello Em.' He looks as shocked to say my name as I am to hear it.

It seems I've been found.

Tower

MY BEST FRIEND Jennifer lived in a concrete tower that was sixteen storeys tall. From her crow's nest bedroom – cosy as a ship's cabin – you could see, way down below, the derelict remains of the old steel city. Her room smelt of the body spray she pinched from her sister, sweet like vanilla and heavy as an ache.

The last time I went for tea, Jenny whined for lasagne, 'like we had at Em's café' (remembering the day my mother dumped us there and we got in the way while dad tried to work). But her mum made us beans on soft white toast and said to me, 'Is your hand better now, love? The bandage is off.' She was asking a kind thing, but it threatened to open a wound that attention would only make deeper. When she dropped me home later, I managed not to let her in.

The Promise

THEY STEPPED OUTSIDE the library and into a slicing wind. Nowhere, Gabriel thought, could the month of February be more bleak than here, in the grim grey north. But he preferred the city draped in darkness and strung with amber lights.

His mother was running late, and for all his self-schooling bravado, he'd rather not suffer the fume-filled busses. Em had a place she could take him to wait. She led him towards the old cathedral where the flagstones were polished by the glare of streetlamps.

'Does your mum know I've been helping you?' she asked as they walked.

'Shit no, she's still freaking out about the home-schooling, I don't want her thinking I'm trying it on with the librarian.' This fear that they shared – of being misunderstood – was inflamed by the strangeness of their friendship: with ten years between them and not a flicker of attraction, it made sense only as a collaboration of curious minds.

'Did you find out what happened to her, after?' Em

quizzed him.

'I'm not sure if it's the right thread to keep following,' he replied.

Their path twisted into an alleyway that he'd never discovered on his lunchtime wanderings, a tight gloomy tunnel with no visible end. Em disappeared through a metal gate in the side of the wall, a tall narrow opening that you wouldn't see if you didn't know it was there. In an unlit stairwell that smelled like urine, she paused to warn him, 'I've never brought anyone else with me, I only come here alone. And while we're in there, don't move stuff around or leave anything behind.'

They wound up a stairway that was close and uneven, two floors, then three, until at the top, she stopped at the dim shape of a door. Unmarked and uninviting – an entrance, or a dead end? Should they really be here? And what was Em doing, was she breaking in? For a moment he hoped so.

But no, because Em had a key, a gift from her father: the power to enter.

'He's closed on Mondays, so it's all ours.'

She unlocked the door and unveiled the sleeping relic of a café. A shipwreck of chairlegs upturned on tables was outlined in halflight, waiting in stillness.

'It's like a hidden cave,' said Gabriel quietly.

'I've brought us up the back way, that's all. From the front it's nothing special.'

She moved with quick confidence, flicking on a lamp and swinging seats to the floor, at ease with their weight despite her own slightness. The light didn't quite reach into the corners and the cold air prickled with the promise of the unseen.

They stayed bundled in coats, wrapped in the smells of well-worn wood and steam from the machine. He didn't drink coffee normally, but was easily persuaded by the tower of wobbling foam she had conjured. *I can tell her*, he thought.

Threshold

I USED TO think that Val was my grandma, and I longed for my Saturday visits to her slanty terraced house on the top of the hill.

In her box of a back yard, the sun made sharp shadows from the corners of the outhouse that used to be a toilet. She fed the birds like they were her babies and introduced me to Perceval the Garrulous, the chattering jay. My own wings uncurled from the knots at my shoulders as I crayoned his feathered portrait, with velvety brown and a piercing blue.

Once, when my mother arrived, we smuggled my drawing of Percey Jay back over the threshold, a secret amulet that Val helped me hide. His picture was folded a hundred times over, to fit him inside my plastic-beaded purse.

I'd also taken a bit of Val's accent home with me that day, like a warm blanket. 'We speak properly in this house Emily, not like your auntie,' my mother said later, as she flicked through magazines that told you how to get the love you deserve.

Thin Air

I SOMETIMES THINK that my mother should have been called Alice, not Veronica.

When she arrives at my top-floor flat, it's as if she's been swigging from the drink-me potion. She's out of control, imposing, unpredictable. Her speech skews into riddle, incomprehensible. My room can't contain it, her unbounded desire for a thing un-nameable, an elusive something that I can never quite grasp for her.

'It's too hot, Emily!' she complains of the coffee I make. (None for me: it would be cold by the time I've made hers right, and found a shallow dish in my non-smoking flat to catch the droppings from her cigarette). 'It's barely a studio really,' she reminds me every visit, dusting the surfaces with the ash of disgrace.

This flat holds me tight, with its matchbox bed and mini kitchenette. But with her here, it starts to feel as intolerable as the coffee.

I move the scalding mug to the table that squats like a toadstool by the reading chair she's landed in. Swallowing the urge to apologise – for water too hot, for the flat's tiny size, for my stupid self – I open the window. But not too much as 'It's freezing in here!' The squeaky old latch isn't loud enough, today, to mask a stranger sound that I hear. A voice at my shoulder that's not my mother, but Gabriel, the kid from the library, I swear, like he's shrunk down to nothing and perched himself there.

'*This isn't who you have to be,*' comes the message from thin air. I shrink away from words that feel like a scratchy label inside my clothes. I'd quite like a spell that would make me smaller, to make enough room for both minding my mother and ignoring this imagined advice.

Val would know what to do. I summon her strength from the other side of the city, remembering the saying that Val tells me was lore. *Up high, you're safe*, they've said this forever. But we're three floors up and though it feels like four, I want to go higher, cross over a threshold, be sent somewhere else. To the tall ancient cedar who stands out there. I could hide in her needles and breathe from her scent, and find in her deep-green fingers a cradle to rest in.

But then who would cool my mother's coffee? And take her to lunch? And share a cringe with the waiter who must – she demands – tend only her. And bear the embarrassment when the salad is wrong (though it's exactly what she ordered), and she asks for prosecco, as if she hasn't already had enough. Who would mend her unending frustrations and make it alright for her to settle, and stop, become playful again?

Sparkling

THERE WAS NO time to gather, to save and protect, when she came flooding into the room. My secret bird-friends lay helpless as paper napkins scattered across the cream carpet. Listing over me, she lifted Percey Jay, his cobalt-crayoned wing shaking in her hand. To steady her, I scrunched him up.

No more Percey Jay.

Now, she was ready to play. On her snow-white bed, she poured out a tangle of chains and gems. My clumsy hot fingers caught on a long-feathered bird. I loved it and it was beautiful and it made me sad. Curled in on itself and twinkling in jade and ultramarine, skewered by a pin through its back. Sparkling and lifeless, imprisoned in glittering form to make my mother shimmer like stardust.

Ten Tall Tales That Gabriel Has Told Me

1. That he escaped the suffocations of school and moved himself here, into the library, where he wanted to learn the things they didn't know, those teachers of syllabus and a dead history.

2. That his age, by years, is only fifteen. But by the memories he sees of flooded destruction, he can only be older, too old to recall how he survived the succumbing to water they were forced to endure. (*Seriously? A young-old boy with past-life memories?*)

3. That he's searching the archives to fill in the gaps, and enlisted his mother to quell her fears of online slacking and qualified-for-nothing.

4. That he dispatched her here, to gather the proof that he's engaged in real study, from proper printed books, their dust covers guarding abandoned treasures.

5. That this is all he wants from me: my help with his quest, my power to free these locked-up truths from the vault of deep exile. (*He must've seen me coming, a*

bored librarian who falls easily for a story, a legend, a lie – these tempting old friends of mine).

6. That he doesn't also hope, secretly, that something will happen between him and me.

7. That he has no clue how he already knew my name, that day in December when instead of his mother, he came to collect the pile of reserved books and records.

8. That he needs to remember – and I need to see – that these stories aren't over, forgotten and done, washed away by our arrogance and the myth that we're safe.

9. That the burden is mine as much as it's his, to recover our cast-off inheritance. He's not being awkward, that's just how it is.

10. That I should believe him, with his trickster's flourish; that I wouldn't be stupid to become enthralled.

Journal of Incalculable Loss, Author Unknown

Record #44203: Extracts from a personal journal, donated to Sheffield City Library Archive

March 12th, 1864

Such dreadful, terrible news! But I shall not be shielded from it! I learned of it from Doctor Beck's newspaper. An incalculable loss of life, yet there are those whose very job it is to count the corpses and record the facts. Drowned in their own beds, some of them! When he left I tried to rest, but all I could hear was the inhuman roar of the water that the survivors had described.

March 16th, 1864

I read today about the 'disaster tourists' who arrive in a daily torrent at the railway station, just as the flood inundated the houses in its path. They come to stare without shame at the gaping holes where once people's lives stood. Like the little girl who escaped unscathed, her entire family – and the first two storeys of the house – swept away from beneath her attic bedroom as she slept.

Betsy acts like we should pretend it has not even happened. Just like she carries on as if Pa were still here: preparing the luncheon and washing the sheets as if nothing has changed. 'I know I am not your mother,' she said this morning, 'and I have never pretended to be, but I will not leave you, and not just because your father left enough for my wage. I won't let you stay shut away up here forever!'

When she eventually went back down to the kitchen, I pulled out the newspaper and read again the story of the girl who survived. I turned to the window, hoping for a flicker of life against the cedar's dark needles, but there was no movement.

<u>*November 2nd, 1864*</u>

The Claims hearings will begin this month. The victims may submit a list of items, to request compensation from the Water Company, for loss of livelihood and belongings. But how can you claim for what cannot be replaced?

One life in a list

Dresses:
floral-patterned linen
with covered buttons;
cotton summer dress
embroidered with daisies;
white-and-green leaf print
with gathered skirt;
mauve silk-satin
in puff sleeve style.

Black leather shoes,
only for best,
worn six times.

Three night-dresses
with lace trim and frills.

Violin in 7/8 size;
case lined in red felt;
bow with ebony heel,
inlaid with mother-of-pearl.

Folding rosewood music stand

*and sheet music collected
from esteemed fiddlers of the north.*

*Notebooks and journals,
some leather-bound,
contents unmemorised.*

*Collection of textbooks:
'The Ecology of Streams'
'Ocean Navigation'
and 'Fauna of the Sea'.*

*Quilt made by hand
from scraps kept and transformed
(a birthday present, twenty-first,
gifted only two seasons ago
by a dear friend now Crossed).*

*Pewter hand mirror
with waterbird relief
over handle and back.*

*Hexagonal trinket box,
bottle-green glass
with polished gold trim.*

*Six-inch hat pin
with a small butterfly
of pale blue enamel.*

*Sterling silver brooch
embellished with motif
of wildflowers
and the name Cecilia.*

Exchange

'I CAN'T BELIEVE I grew up here, and never knew,' I say to Gabriel. I'm still taking it in, the foundation of loss that this city sits upon. I've brought him to the café while it's closed, so we can go over in it private.

Compulsively, he regurgitates the tragic reports from the sea of papers spread all around us. 'The Great Sheffield Flood,' he repeats, 'Two hundred and forty, all drowned in one night. Do you think they felt it coming?'

His discovery pulls uncomfortably at something drawn tight inside me. An echo of pity stirs in the depths of my body, or memory, and I catch myself. What right do I have to feel the stab of this pain inside my own chest? I steer us back to the facts we've collected, a collage of fragments, bits of lives inundated.

'So what d'you reckon, this is what you've been seeing?' I ask. His visions have risen from a place unknown. The more he's told me, the more real it becomes. The first time he spilled it – his hallucinated secret – he worried it sounded like the symptoms of illness, the seeing of things that can't have happened to him. But he knows they are true.

'I don't think that this is the flood that I've seen. The tide is bigger, the water seems higher, if that's possible. And later on, after – it doesn't go down. Things don't return to how they had been, like they were before.' He starts gathering and piling up the copies of records and books and his notes. 'Maybe all this was a fucking waste of time. I'm so sorry, Em, I thought it made sense.'

'It does though,' I tell him, 'I'm glad that I know about these people, their lives and their deaths. It matters, even if it doesn't match what you thought it meant.' He seems defeated, stranded among the empty tables and upturned chairs and I want to throw him a rope. It comes out by accident – an offering, disclosure, a piece of my failure to make him feel better. 'I was married,' I drop into the pool of quiet. 'I was twenty-four, it lasted less than a year.'

'I'm sorry,' he says, and I'm sideswept again by how mature he seems. Not like me, twenty-five and shipwrecked in my own humiliation.

It must have worked: he's got that look, a glint of provocation, nudging me towards the limits of acceptance. 'I see you,' he says, and I hope he's switching topic. 'But when we're not together, like when you're at home. Oh – no, not in a creepy way, I don't mean like that,' he scrambles for clarity.

But it's okay.

'I hear you,' I say, meaning something beyond not doubting his memories. 'I hear your voice, when you're not there,' I admit.

What I want – though I don't dare – is to ask him,
What do you see,
when you see me?

Small Hope

LOOK AWAY, SAYS the nurse's face as it falls into serious.

There's nothing to see, an invisible injury. How stupid I was, to hope that I'd leave with a photo and a belly full of promise.

Look away, their faces say, the women waiting their turn. Uncontrolled loss can be dangerous.

How stupid I was, not to have sensed it wasn't there anymore. How careless of me, to have lost my baby and not even known. Like a bag of shopping dropped on the way home, the one with the sugar that can't be replaced, or faked.

Look away, I should know, to make my pain small. Untroublesome as the day they stitched my wound at the children's hospital.

Look away, look away. So you won't see me.

Part Two

Spellbroken

HE'S AWAKE BEFORE any light touches the walls of his tiny cell, before the clattering bell that tells them when to rise, when to eat, when to work and when to sleep. He has just spent his last night in this narrow bed. Today, his confinement is over, and he'll be free to leave.

He is not sure if he wants that freedom.

He'll be expected, soon, in Jed's office, the only place it's possible to escape the nauseating smell of tea tree oil. Jed's room is as small as the ones they sleep in, but it has a window onto the mountain. The low sofa makes it feel like therapy, no matter how many times Jed protests that it isn't. Jed will want to know – did he get what he came for? And how will he reply? That he didn't come to get enlightened, or to advance his practice. He just wanted to be left the hell alone.

Would he confess that sometimes – when they were all in the hall, sitting in busy stillness and waiting for transformation – he'd sneak off alone, out onto the hillside? Where he's gathered into a spell cast by the resin of juniper and the resting pause of hawkmoth. A hidden realm, silent and singing. Peaceful as an underwater world, inside which he's invisible and infinite.

No. He'll preserve those rare and fathomless moments, keep them unlabelled, unliked, unspoiled.

As he descends the mountain, his old friend the wind slips under his bones, and opens his wings onto a pillow of air. His earth-bound form is released, a wild streak of blue feather merging into oceanic sky.

Crush

FUCK YOU, I curse internally. I'm trying something new in the studio today. *Fuck you, Gabriel*, I think, not saying it out loud, *you wouldn't even find me at the library now.*

The other students are all way younger than me, a sad late-starter pushing thirty. My carry-case is spotless as new white trainers; theirs are battered with the splashes and spills of proper artists. My head hurts from concentrating, or from my too-tight ponytail. I tell myself I'm only giving this a go for Val. Not for myself.

At the start of the class, I listened hard to Leo (short for Leonella, never Miss Faresi, this isn't high school). Her silver-stroked hair was half loose, brushing her shoulders as she talked about emotions, and how they have colours.

I don't get it.

THE MUSIC LEO has put on is dark and lonely and it pulls something out of me that I heave up and out onto the canvas. A gash of electric blue. It's the colour of an old eyeshadow I found in mum's jewelbox, in a little round pot, the pigment dense as soot.

Fuck you mother, my mind tries on for size, as I unleash a flood of the shocking blue. Then start to cover it with lavender and translucent pale grey. Strokes of thistle-purple form a whorl like a snail's shell. When I was little, I would watch the snails slide across our garden path, imperial shells held high. I wanted to catch that moment, when they knew, to pull inside. One sunlit afternoon I almost saw it. But my mother squashed it with a stumble of her stiletto-heeled boot.

'Hmmm...' I hear from behind me: Leo, preparing to comment. My shoulders cramp tight as I wait till she's here, with me, beside me, in front of my work. Her warm bare arms are strong, the skin satin-brown like the bark of a mature tree.

'Yes, Em' she says. 'But don't control yourself so much.' Soaked in her attention, I feel guilty and brazen. I may as well lift up my skirt and flash everyone my knickers.

BY THE END of the class, the canvas mirrors back a mosaic of messy pieces. Shards of myself, rudely shaken free.

    screaming magenta

        intense indigo

    sky-blue possibility

        mournful deep turquoise

    trembling sea-green

The image resolves to an uncontained storm. Tempestuous waves, white edges sharp as broken glass. I fear I've gone too far.

Hush

ON THE DAY of Val's funeral it's unusually hot. In my parents' garden, the scent of dry heat bounces off baked concrete. The guests gather on the bristly shaved grass, their stiff elderly legs holding them aloof from the thirsty earth beneath. They're listening to my mother who is swaying slightly on a patch of polished stone, the faux-palms behind her almost static in their pots.

'Some of you you know she was a mother to me really ... I don't know how to do all the ... when I was little she would always tell me you know ... that's not right ... I hope you all stay for some food ... no no not inside the new patio she didn't like –'

From my perch at the top of the back steps, I unfreeze and fly down to intervene. I take away my mother's drink and steer her to a sheltered corner, underneath the heavy blooming lilac. The gaggle of mourners relax and begin to mingle, like currents in a human tide.

Bracing myself, I notice an uninvited guest edging towards us, a colourful jay gripping the tightrope fence with his delicate talons. It's the second time in two days that I've been pulled out of the blackness – momentarily – by that streak of unexpected blue. Yesterday at Val's, I'd abandoned the crushing weight of sorting through her things, and curled into the old swivel chair, wanting to sleep off my grief. But a shadow-feathered reflection kept scratching outside the window, the incessant tapping of beak on pane sounding out my name, 'Em, Em, Em.'

Under the heads of nodding lilac, my mother lurches a little. Her alcoholic fumes thicken in the airless heat, trapping us both. 'You never went!' I lash out, clawing for freedom. 'You never came to Auntie Val's. So, okay, you went. But you never came *in*, not properly. Every Saturday-'

'But you loved being there!' she flares unstably.

'And she loved having me,' I persist, 'but where were *you*? You don't even know these people. Two busses, for most of them, to get all the way out here. And you're acting like you're the only person-'

'Stop it Emily, you can be so nasty. You know I can't cope with this. Not today, with my anxiety. It's too hot, I need to go inside, can you get your dad.' He's all the way up the steps, hiding behind a tray of full glasses.

'*You* wanted to do this outside!' I challenge, reckless. And then pay the price. My mother's lean goes on for too long, turning into a collapse that will be seen by everyone. I'm forced to become the safety net, spreading myself out invisibly thin to catch her, to hush her panic and my own rising anger.

    I get her inside, away from concerned eyes. Relief trickles through me. It won't be today. When I have to feel the pain of stretching the unused parts of myself.

Inheritance

IT WASN'T VERONICA'S fault.

That her medication made her so woozy. That she didn't know what to say to those people outside on her lawn.

That Val had got lumbered looking after her, the two of them stuck in that cold damp terrace, where the stench of the outside toilet clung to everything, even though it hadn't been in use for years.

Veronica feels Emily watching her from the bedroom doorway, giving her that look. As if Veronica doesn't fit properly, in this spacious white room. The double-glazing muffles the abrasive rumbling of passing cars, but not Emily's harshness when she says, 'I thought you wanted to lie down.'

'I just want to find something first,' Veronica replies. The disapproval is an echo of the accusation that hung unspoken in the children's A&E – how many years back now? – when the nurse was stitching up Emily's hand. *How could she not have seen the wine glass, right there in the sink?*

Defiantly, Veronica reaches into the top shelf of the built-in wardrobe. She lifts down the wooden jewelbox that they once both loved and drops it onto the creamy pillowy duvet. They sit close together on the bed as Veronica tries to open the box. Her fingers are shaking so much that Emily takes over, strangling the sparkle of anticipation.

Veronica pulls at a dull silver chain. On the end of it, a small purple oval dangles between them. The smooth egg-shape is split into halves by a hinge, the solid amethyst shattered by crackles running through it like veins of bright trapped rage.

'Remember this?' Veronica asks.

'Auntie Val's locket.'

'I never told her I had it, because then she'd know I used to skip school, when our dad still had his job. She'd have been so cross.'

It hadn't even been Veronica who'd found the locket, but her nosy friend Susie when she tugged at Val's bedspread and it tumbled out with a photo of a woman, wearing the same purple pebble pressed into her heart.

Veronica had lied.

She did that a lot. She lied to the teachers when they asked how the girls were coping. She lied to her classmates about her second-hand coat. She lied to Susie about the photo that couldn't have been her mother, because her mother never smiled like that.

'You don't know, Emily, what it's like, growing up without proper hot water or enough money for school shoes.' Veronica feels brave, saying these things that she's tried to pretend were not real. Her daughter's chest sinks in a disbelieving sigh.

Emily would never know what it was like. To have to hide it from people, the truth of what you lived in. That you didn't deserve nice things like everyone else.

'You can have the locket, Emily. I just wanted my turn. Do what you want. Wear it, or put it away.' *Or break it – I don't care,* Veronica lies to herself.

Homecoming

ONE DARK MORNING, he follows me to the red-brick sanctum of the art school, where I draw and paint and rage, hemmed in by human chatter.

When we scatter after class, released by the rotating door, I see him on the steps below. He's waited there all day, in the weak winter light, his claws pressed as in prayer to the cold hard stone. I hear him call my name, 'Em.'

Again.

Like he did when I was little, and I had to choose between the boundless realms that beckoned me and my mother's grasping terror.

Like he did when he first came back, in the body of a teenage boy, intruding with no apology on the riskless peace of the library.

Like he did when his bodiless voice slipped inside my head, seeding unwanted truths that I tried to keep buried.

Like he did when he returned with wings, crashing into Val's window and stalking her funeral.

Like he has the whole time he's waited, outside my

home, calling to me from his perch in the prickly green cedar. Declaring his devotion, his desire to protect, the pain he has shared watching me wade through sorrow, and his joy – how *dare* he! – at what he calls my shedding of disguise.

For years he's been gone. He never returned – the Gabriel who set off for a two-week retreat, remote but supposedly brief. He left me sunk on my own in the loneliness of losing Val. And he thinks he can turn up now, shifted in shape, expecting us to be friends like before.

When he speaks my name again as we stand frozen on the steps, I pretend I can't hear him. As if he really is just a jay with an odd-sounding squawk. I shoo him away.

BUT HE COMES back again, forceful as my mother is fragile. He taps on my black gabled window and tells me
what he sees,
when he sees me.

Beyond

WE'RE STARING AT my painting, pondering the flood. The canvas dominates the space in my overstuffed flat, sweeping aside even my toadstool table. Percey perches there, his scaled feet drawing a scratchy tune from the small circle of wood. Next to my painting – a violent expansion of restless deep ocean – his own jay's feather is a borrowed scrap of blue.

'Em, look!' he says. In the centre of the crushing water and hissing spray, he sees a figure, 'sitting in stillness, gathering power. Look Em, *there*.'

A heron?

Or a woman?

'She's gone Beyond,' he pronounces. 'Where she's gone, the air sparkles with aliveness and the colours sing, fierce and bright–'

'Percey, don't start,' I roll my eyes at his lyrical flight. He tips his beak to the cracks in the ceiling, following my gaze with his refusal to yield to my harsh human cynicism.

'I can take you there,' he tries, baiting me with outlandish fantasy.

'Come on Em,' he goads, with a flash of juvenile arrogance. Folding his soft brown wings, his eyes land hard on mine and he says, 'You can see her.'

I can't.

Maybe the painting is like those pictures of the maiden and the crone. The ones that change when you open your gaze just wide enough to expose the illusion. I know what Percey wants from me.

But it's not so simple. Not even in those poisoned spaces online, where they call them out – people like my mum and dad – calling them Refusers. The judgemental label makes me think of all the refuse my parents have shed, over the years, like unwanted skin: the empty packaging from all the shiny things that were supposed to bring them joy and security and love.

It never worked for my mother. The five-bed house, the new-wardrobe-every-season, the Mother's Day jewellery, the summer villa-with-a-pool… None of it steadied her, or repaired her frailty. *Of course* she's refusing to board one of the rafts: she can barely cope with life on land. *I* can't persuade her that the only real choice is a mirage of refuge, beyond the edge of safety.

Dad's no help. When we talk alone, he concedes it does seem possible, the drowning of the cities. Then he goes and hides at the café, serving last meals as if his customers are going on holiday. At home with my mother he continues the pretense (he's well practised) that everything is ok.

Normal.

A dream we have clung to and hidden behind, wishing it into fanciful reality.

Percey's mission is to pop that bubble – pecking and prodding me to embrace an impossibility. I go rigid in protest, my body as brittle as ice.

All I can see in the middle of the storm is a woman left drowning, because I gave up trying to save her. My choice in this moment is to submit to the bracing in my belly, let it encase me in a cage that's as stubborn as diamonds.

Surrender

Too tired of resisting,
I've invited him in.
Let his wings expand
my chest and my vision,
let his voice plant into me
the seeds of rebellion.

A roar in my belly
propels me upwards
and breaks me apart,
birthing me bigger
and pulling me together.

I reach out sideways
as my own wings
stretch
open.

There is no ground
beneath me:
I have left
the world I know.

Part Three

Creation

This is what she sang to me,
the story of creation:

For many many years,
in the unseen darkness,
something frightening was growing.

She pushed it down
into formless blackness,
a weight that she carried,
monstrosity kept cloistered.

She tried to hold it,
all that was too much,
so that we could dance
free from our own pain.

But we were not dancing.
And it was poisoning her.

To begin with
she cried
at the wretched futility
of agony ignored.

*But then it grew teeth
and tore at her
until she exploded,
howling and screeching,
quenching our protests
that nothing was wrong.*

*For a moment she collapsed
into a release
that blanketed her rage.*

*Until new waves
began building
in her amniotic depths,
one behind the other.*

*With each one that peaked,
she purged our pollution
in a vomit of cleansing.*

*Messy.
Necessary.*

This is what she sings to me still,
lulling me into her fierce embrace.

She sings of how
she bore this for us,

*the two-legged beings
who call her destructive,
even as we fill her
with our offloaded shame.
We, the land-dwellers*

*cowering behind barriers
as her bloody floods break.*

*We, the beings paralysed
by our unspoken dread
that it might be our fault.*

*We, the refugees
who seek a groundless home
upon her salty heaving breast.*

She sings to me now
of how tenderly she will hold us
as we weep together
in our surrender to the sea.

Our separation will be severed
as we emerge,
fragile and unsteady,
into the vital chaos
of the new life
we have incubated.

Volunteers Needed:
Must be willing to tend pain

I FIND HER at home, this last Saturday morning that my feet will feel the firm kiss of concrete. Despite the unworldly heat, the windows are shut, the air close and sickly.

'You're being very selfish Emily,' my mother greets me. She reaches for the glass that stands loyally on the table next to the sofa. She'll have taken her pills well before she got started on the vodka. I hope. Sitting there, she looks childish and small, washed up on an island of cushioned beige.

I try not to think about where might be safe anymore. Not since the domes of the shopping centre were claimed by the water.

'I'm going to *help* people,' I rise to my own defence.

But I wonder if she's right.

Is that why I gave dad my painting of the storm? Not just to remember me by, but to cover up my guilt. Nailed to the wall of his empty café-in-the-attic, it's no substitute for my presence. It's hard to tell if it's the truth he's avoiding, or my mother's lounging denial.

As she leans across the sofa, my mother knocks her glass flying and I catch it with a flinch-quick reflex. 'I'll make you a coffee,' I say, to anchor myself.

After I'm done here, I have one more stop: auntie Val's old terrace, up on the hill where the lightning struck.

I used to be able to keep my own pain tucked away. When the baby was gone, it seemed easy to let people tell me it happened for a reason, that it wasn't yet a person. But when Val died it was like having a bandage ripped off before the bleeding has stopped.

The thought of her is an undertow that rocks my shaky steadiness. A welcome ache floods my throat and fills the kitchen until I cradle the feeling like a tender purple bruise. Painful and beautiful.

I want to feel the same precious grief for my mother. Only, I don't seem to feel *anything* properly inside the radius of her relentless distress. I can't exactly blame her. For the drinking, or the lashing out. For how she's constructed a fortress no less wobbly than a stack of wooden blocks.

But I can't risk hiding in this sinking broken city, no matter how savage the self-judgement that nips at me. They're building something, out there on the ocean. Tomorrow, my pushy friend Percey will take me to the shrinking edge of the shore, the edge of my fear, and remind me there's no going back on my promise.

Before I leave, I set down the coffee on the table by my mother. Her head has dropped forwards, fallen into a midday slumber. In spite of the urge to rouse her (just enough to comfort myself), I don't try to wake her.

Temporary Safety

THIS GIRL COULD be me, was my unspoken thought as she boarded my raft for the ceremony. We were well beyond any sight of land. The slimy deck croaked underfoot, and she gripped my arm tight even though I'm the elder.

They expect some sort of oracle, these young renunciates. I might be old, but I'm no wiser than she, my next partner in this eternal monthly cycle. Generation Compensation, we used to call them in training: burning with eco-fervour, fuelled by guilt for harms that were done before they were even born.

Today the ocean is quiet, having cried herself down into drowsy relief. The first storm this month was a fierce one. We were diverted last night to temporary shelter at *Éa Cleafa**, the great pseudo-anchor, built to make hope feel solid.

Some people feel safer in a torrent of commotion, lashed to their refuge, than when they are free in the deep confronting silence.

I was alone on deck when the gull brought the news. Seven lost this time. One of them mine. 'Not yours,' his correction was swift as a slap from his wing. But an affectionate one. My job is not to save, only to tend.

The lost woman I'd tended was known as Danula. The gull told how she held firm at her station during the storm, devoted weather-dreamer, stayed till the stilts were ripped from the seabed and her body dragged under the depths that cushion my craft. The sardines we pull out will always taste faintly of the death that feeds them. As the gull departed westward, I scattered Dani's memory into the jewel-clear sky, edgeless as her spirit.

My current charge will depart at the end of this moon, taking her heartbreak with her. The storm has made it heavier, and angrier, the fermenting weight that will eventually transform her.

* From the Old English *Éa,* meaning river or running water and *Cleafa*, meaning cleaved, 'that which is separated', or chamber.

The Crossing

THE CAVE-BLACK NIGHT holds a bright half moon: a humbling setting for their secluded ritual. Even up on the sloping deck, the raft smells of seaweed and undried wood. They sit like a pair of salt-kissed seals, warming themselves by the leaping fire and feeling the pull of the ocean current, deep in their guts.

Cecily picks up her list, ready to begin. Her eyes (unlike Em's) are sharp enough to read by the shapeshifting flames. Each item is declared aloud, her inventory ticked off into the listening air. She speaks of no devices: she must have shed her digital skin long before her training began. Her phone was not the hardest thing to let go of. But Em is curious about the brooch. 'Is that your full name – Cecilia?' she asks.

'No, it's just Cecily, but I found that second-hand, and thought it could be me.'

So many people smuggle these in, the manufactured reminders stashed inside their single bag, a piece they've saved from a life so precarious. Em feels the small weight that hangs at her own chest, smooth as a bird's egg: an amethyst memorial to the ties she's broken. Cecily is unburdened by even the tiniest trinket. Born into catastrophe, a primal force drives her, and will bear her patiently over the Crossing.

The Crossing is not a place (they discover), not a somewhere to get to. It's a space. Merged with sea and sky, an impossible vastness that can hold the blossoming of grief and courage.

Cecily says, 'The jewellery and clothes, that was just stuff. But the violin, she was kind of a friend.' Em knows what she means.

When the water first started rising, they thought they could just go higher. But they couldn't go high enough. The birds knew first, and they all left, except for the guides who stayed to help, and the gulls who came inland to escort them away from their tethered security. The volunteers like Em. Sometimes, when she scans for the last scraps of land, her painter's eye embroiders blue feather, or the tip of a cedar.

She see only blackness now, and the brilliance of the fire as it consumes the list, along with who Cecily was. Gently, the breeze takes the ashes they offer and clothes them both in a layer of elemental dust.

***

ON THE DAWN of full moon, they are woken by the clunk and slop of Guillame and his boat. He is Cecily's ride to

Éa Cleafa, the great floating refuge.

In the womb of the Crossing, Cecily's guarded self has died. She has befriended the rawness of rage, swum unhindered into the terror of sadness. She has tasted rich stillness, the truth of no hope. Now she can go further.

She casts off, leaving behind Em's raft – its own small island, rocked by the ocean and weathered by the wind, strong and exposed to the wild inbetween. There, Em waits. Tending fire, with the moon-on-the-wane.

The Authors

David Rhymes

David Rhymes lives in Navarra, Spain. He grew up in Nottingham and has a degree in English Literature from the University of Warwick and an MA in Creative Writing from the University of East Anglia. He earns his living as a freelance translator, trainer, and instructional designer.

His fiction has appeared in the Bath Flash Fiction, Reflex Fiction and Fish Publishing anthologies, and has won prizes in the Bath Flash Fiction and Barren Magazine competitions. Other short listings include the Bridport, LISP, Desperate Literature and Smokelong Quarterly flash fiction competitions.

Hannah Sutherland

Hannah's novel was longlisted in Helen Lederer's Comedy Women in Print Award in the unpublished category, she was Highly Commended in the Bridport Prize for her short story, and she won Cranked Anvil's flash fiction competition. Her Novella-in-Flash, *Small Things*, was Highly Commended in the Bath Novella in Flash Award and was published by Ad Hoc Fiction. She has recent writing published in Ellipsis Zine and Litro.

Dawn Siofra North

Dawn Siofra North is part of a home-educating family, an occasional mindfulness teacher and a writer of tiny stories. Her work has been shared in *Legerdemain* (National Flash Fiction Day Anthology 2021) and on the *Free Flash Fiction* website. She is inspired by story-based learning and imaginative meditation.

Manufactured by Amazon.ca
Bolton, ON